MW00711239

Philippines

Luzon
Strait

Cordillera
Administrative
Region (or CAR)

BABUYAN
ISLANDS

Philippine
Sea

ILOCOS
NORTE APAYAO
CAGAYAN
Ilocos Vigan ABRA Tuguegarao
KALINGA
ILOCOS MT.
SUR PROVINCE Ilagan
LA UNION IFUGAO ISABELA
San Fernando NUEVA
BENGUET VIZCAYA
QUIRINO
PANGASINAN

Cagayan
Valley

Central
Luzon

NUEVA Baler
TARLAC ECIJA AURORA
ZAMBALES
PAMPANGA
Central BULACAN
Luzon BATAAN Manila RIZAL
CAVITE Polillo
National Capital LAGUNA
Region (or NCR) BATANGAS
QUEZON

CALABARZON

CAMARINES Bicol
NORTE
CAMARINES CATANDUANES
SUR Virac
MARIN- ALBAY
DUQUE
Mamburao SORSOGON
OCCIDENTAL ORIENTAL
MINDORO MINDORO
NORTHERN
SAMAR
ROMBLON Masbate
SAMAR
MASBATE
Western AKLAN BILIRAN
Visayas CAPIZ EASTERN
ANTIQUE ILOILO SAMAR
San Jose Bago Tacloban
GUIMARAS LEYTE
CEBU SOUTHERN SURIGAO
NEGROS LEYTE DEL NORTE
OCCIDENTAL
NEGROS Surigao
Central ORIENTAL Northern
Visayas SIQUIJOR CAMIGUIN Mindanao AGUSAN
MISAMIS DEL NORTE
MISAMIS ORIENTAL Prosperidad AGUSAN
ZAMBOANGA OCCIDENTAL DEL SUR
DEL NORTE LANAO BUKID-
Zamboanga DEL NORTE NON DAVAO
Peninsula ZAMBOANGA LANAO
SIBUGAY DEL SUR COMPOSTELA
ZAMBOANGA Cotabato VALLEY
DEL SUR SHARIFF COTABATO
Zamboanga KABUN- Davao DAVAO
SUAN MAGUIN- Digos ORIENTAL
BASILAN DANAO
SULTAN
Jolo KUDARAT SOUTH Davao
SULU COTABATO Region
SOCCSKSARGEN SARANGANI DAVAO
DEL SUR

MIMAROPA

PALAWAN

South
China
Sea

Puerto
Princesa

Sulu

Sea

Eastern
Visayas

EASTERN
SAMAR
Tacloban
LEYTE

TYPHOON
YOLANDA

Caraga

SURIGAO
DEL SUR

Kota Belud

Sandakan

MALAYSIA

Muslim Mindanao
(or ARMM)
TAWI-TAWI

Celebes Sea

ar Seri
wan

Bangar

INDONESIA

0 50 100 150 Kilometers
0 50   100   150 Miles

ORSOGON NORTHERN
SAMAR
Eas
SAMAR Vis
LIRAN EASTERN
SAMAR
Tacloban
LEYTE
BU SOUTHERN SURI
LEYTE DEL

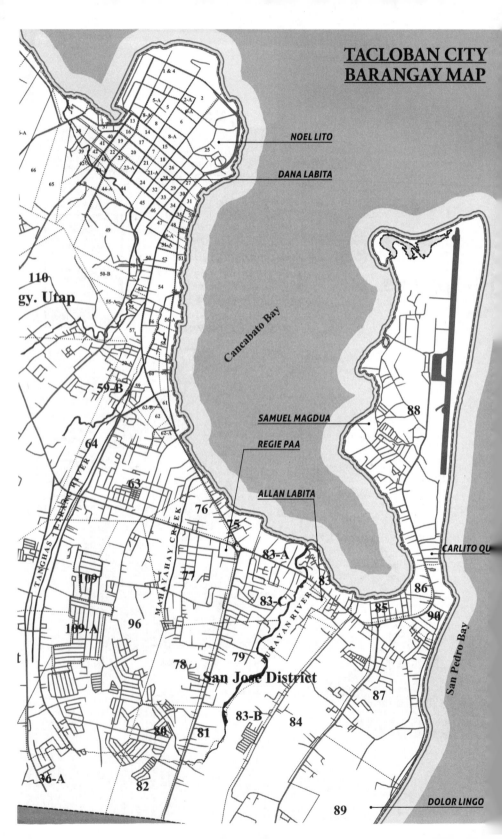

TACLOBAN CITY BARANGAY MAP

NOEL LITO

DANA LABITA

Cancabato Bay

SAMUEL MAGDUA

REGIE PAA

ALLAN LABITA

CARLITO QU

DOLOR LINGO

110
gy. Utap

59-B

64

63

76

75

83-A

83

86

85

90

83-C

109

77

96

109-A

79

78   San Jose District

87

80   81   83-B   84

36-A

82

89

San Pedro Bay

MATIYAYAHAY CREEK

BURAYAN RIVER

TANGHAS TETRAH RIVER

"... the three Spanish 't's': trabajo [work], techo [roof] and tierra [land]. The Church teaches that every person has the right to these three t's."

—Pope Francis
as reported by, Straatnieuws street magazine,
Netherlands

This book is dedicated to the survivors of Typhoon Yolanda [Haiyan], and to all the marginalized people of the Philippines who do not have jobs, homes and gardens.

It is specifically dedicated to the seven survivors who shared their stories with me: Regie, Carlito, Dana, Dolor, Noel, Samuel and Allan. Theirs are actual stories, based on real experiences and real people. Only Noel's name has been changed. At the time of this writing he is still a fugitive from the law.

ACKNOWLEDGEMENT

Thank you to the incredible people I was surrounded with and supported by, in Tacloban. My wife Deborah, a photographer, who spent three months with me after the typhoon, feeding, caring and sharing the pain of Yolanda's survivors. The three friends we lived with for weeks on end: Sel, Chris and Jake. The Kids International Team: The Long Family, John, Richard and Janet, Reah, Pauline, Pastor Hugh, Norman and the hundreds of others who came and served.

Thank you to the survivors of Typhoon Haiyan, who worked alongside of us tirelessly and sacrificially: Paul, Bon, Alvin, Tina, Ruth, Honey, Pastor Ging, Mel, Beryl, Aira, Abi and many others too numerous to mention.

Thank you to those we partnered with: The Palami Family, The Palami Foundation, the Palo Baptist Church, STEFTI School (the St. Therese Educational Foundation of Tacloban, Inc.), the Navigators, and the 100 plus schools and churches we worked alongside.

Thank you also to my friends, who read, edited and critiqued this manuscript: Michael, Mickey, Pauline, Deborah, Jimbo, my sister Ann, and a special thanks to mother Iris.

— William Shaw

TABLE OF CONTENTS

Chapter 4 – A Sea of Sand

"We get the best and the worst here," he said. "We get you who are helping and we get those who charge too much for coconut lumber." And then he went on to tell us about the storm. "I was eight when MacArthur landed in Palo, Leyte, where I lived and grew up. This typhoon was worse in every way. There was more death, more destruction. The trees snapped like toothpicks." He held up his finger and snapped it shut to show me. "And the ground was like a bald man." He reminisced, his eyes wandering, and his mind going back sixty-nine years to 1944, when Palo was the center of the great war. In his lifetime, in a city with a history of typhoons, WWII was the closest correlation to the reality he was now part of. The violence and annihilation of 1944 had been eclipsed.

—From an aid worker's journal, 2014, Tacloban, Philippines

CHAPTER 1

An Uncertain Calm

SAMUEL MAGDUA

The fish are unloaded and sold in the Tacloban city market just after 4:00 am and then the fishermen motor their boats across the different bays to their homes scattered along the inlets and shores of Eastern Leyte. Forty-nine-year-old Samuel Magdua started fishing thirteen hours earlier, at 5:00 pm, sailing out Baybay past Palo, past Red Beach, past Tanauan, to the Leyte Gulf. He threw his twelve-meter nets, heavy with weights, into the sea and fished for twelve hours, his head resting on his chest, almost asleep. The ocean was calm. There was a *patingalon* moon, just a thin shadow in the sky. The catch was small, but this was not unusual. Samuel understood the moons and the winds. A full moon and there are many fish; after a full moon the fish are gone. All evening and night he trawled the ocean, fishing as he always fished, the water inches away.

He sold his small catch of mixed fish for five hundred pesos, only a fifty-peso profit for his night's work, but Samuel also saved four kilos of shrimp for his and his brother Henry's family to share later in the day.

Samuel's home is built on the western shore of Cancabato Bay, in San Jose, Barangay 88. San Jose sits on a thin finger of a peninsula with two bulbous knuckles. Barangay 88 is on one of the knuckles. It is adjacent to the Daniel Z. Romualdez Airport. The Romualdez family owns the land Samuel lives on, land the Romualdez's or their relatives likely inherited four hundred years before from Spain, as if Spain owned it. But Samuel couldn't care less. He has lived here a lifetime. That this knuckle of land is now swollen with people does not worry him either. His wife is waiting on the shore coffee in her hand. There is a peacefulness in the early morning. The stirring of the neighbors has begun. The dogs are sleeping after a night of barking. The wind blows a cool breath of sea air into the homes. The sun is rising behind him where he and his boat form silhouettes gliding to meet the shore. He drags the rough-hewn keel of his boat across the black sand to safety.

There is a *Kanaway* wind blowing from the west, known to him and his father before him as the most traitorous of winds. For forty-one years he fished these waters. From the days of "no long pants," (something as an eight year-old boy he never wore and never saw) he's been experiencing ocean winds. He knew a *Kanaway* wind brought a low-pressure system and when coupled with an *Anaway* wind, would twist it northerly into a typhoon. He knew a typhoon was predicted, but he was not fishing tonight. He was spending the day drinking *tuba* (coconut wine) with his wife.

Twice in the past Samuel fished in typhoons: Typhoon Ondoy and Typhoon Pablo. Fish prices double after typhoons and successful fishermen take these chances. In Typhoon Pablo his boat almost swamped and as he fought to keep it upright he screamed and shouted at the wind until his voice was hoarse. He defied Pablo and lived, but he defied it knowingly. He knew his path and knew Pablo's path and the paths did not intersect. The coming typhoon, the one reported, would cross any fisherman's path leaving Cancabato Bay.

It was a beautiful Thursday morning. Other boats drifted in. His wife Geraldine handed him coffee. She reached up and brushed her hand on his cowlick and nestled up next to his side. Samuel's hair is thick and bristly black. His body is compact and powerful from years of slapping the water and pulling nets. His sloping shoulders obscure his strength. His face is masked with salt burnt skin. His eyes are dark. There is a shadowy grimness about him, but his white teeth flash, like the diamond in his ear, when he smiles.

A small number of fishermen grouped around. Few words were said. Everyone had just worked a long shift on the sea. In the last twenty years the changes have not been good for fishermen such as Samuel, who trawl within twenty kilometers of the shore.

"Good catch?" someone asked.

Samuel shrugged and held up his bag of undersized shrimp. "We'll eat," he said.

"The typhoon is scaring the fish," another fisherman said.

"The fish have been scared for years," Samuel said. He sipped his coffee and looked at the sea.

"Any sign of the typhoon?" the other fisherman asked.

"Just the *Kanaway*," Samuel replied

The morning talk was muted, both by the catch and by the weather. A super typhoon was predicted. Samuel pulled his boat farther up the shore in preparation for later in the day when it would be secured and sheltered from the coming storm. Other men followed his example.

His neighbor Imbit's boat floated in. Imbit's twelve-year-old boy was with him. Young boys are still fishing. Samuel knows it is against regulations, but who is he to judge. No one in the community criticizes Imbit. Samuel thought of his one child, six-year-old Sheila Mae. God has given him a single child in twenty years. He accepts this, but it saddens him too. All his brothers have more children. Samuel watched Imbit's son, so like himself three decades ago. "If I had a son he would not be fishing. He would be in school, like Sheila Mae. His young hands would not be rough from salt and rope," he said to himself.

Imbit and his son pulled in their boat, but not so far as Samuel.

"Catch was small," said Imbit. Which meant to anyone who knew him it was too small for his family. Imbit's family was big. He had six children and his mother lived with them too.

"I may fish tonight?" said Imbit.

No one answered him. It was a question they all asked and each answer was individual, balanced between need and risk. Each man had his own scale. Each weighed it silently.

Samuel considered Imbit's question. In the village there were two types of fishermen—the "tough guys" and the "rascals." The tough guys were respected, even revered. They were serious fishermen who went out in all weather and all seasons. They faced the perils of sea, which were more than wind and waves, but also pirates and ferries, with a wary acceptance, falling somewhere between self reliance and faith. Their engines were cared for and their nets in order. The "rascals" were the careless ones and those who ran from their responsibilities. Imbit was a respected one.

Samuel remembered when he and his cousin Mario were fishing in the Leyte Gulf. It was early morning, before the sun lit the sky. The net was in the water. The boat drifted. He and Mario rested and then dozed off. Samuel was startled awake with a spear pricking his chest and five pirates with guns and machetes standing over him. He and Mario were prodded off into the sea where they treaded water for three hours. A passing fisherman rescued them. Someone found his boat the following day, drifting in the current, the nets and engine gone.

There was another time a passenger ferry had run down Samuel and his father. At the last minute they had leaped off the dugout and watched the ferry split their boat like an old coconut shell.

"You're lucky," the family had told Samuel's father.

"Miscommunication, the pilot was insane," was all his father would say.

Tragedies at the sea made tough guys and Samuel was one, but he was not fishing tonight; that was decided. Imbit could do as he chose.

"Have you sold the fish?" Geraldine, his wife, was anxious as always.

"Of course," Samuel replied.

"Do you have enough money to buy food?"

Samuel ignored her and walked the forty meters to his home.

Geraldine trailed behind.

At 9:00 am Samuel started his drinking spree. A day to watch TV, talk to the guys and drink his good *tuba* was a day he could love. It was good wine, one hundred and thirty pesos for a gallon compared to the cheap stuff of eighty pesos. Samuel sat back and drank wine. This was the kind of day that his educated brothers often had, but for a fisherman who needed to fish, it was rare.

Samuel watched TV. Initially the weather did not concern him. His boat was secure. He had washed, polished and oiled his engine, a diesel 16hp Japanese machine. His house was strong. He spoke *Waray*, so the English words the announcers kept using on TV, "storm surge," meant nothing to him. Neither he nor Geraldine paid much attention to it.

The day wandered on. He grilled fish. He ate rice. He monitored the storm. A "super" typhoon they kept saying.

"It is too big," he told Geraldine at one point. "I don't like its direction."

"What will happen to us?" she asked.

"Nothing, this is our life."

"Is there something we should do?"

"What can we do? We will wake up again."

"Well, we need money for school for Sheila Mae." The issue of the money from the night's catch was not resolved and this was their constant battle. Samuel would give money, but invariably he kept some back for gambling or drinking.

"I have given you money yesterday."

"It was a very small amount of money."

"Where did it go? Where are you putting the money?"

"I can hardly manage. What is being saved for your habit?"

"There is no money in my pocket. Look," and Samuel emptied a pocket to show her, but he didn't empty them all.

"There are too many things to buy, it makes me angry."

"Don't be angry at me or I will get out of the house," which was a threat and an excuse. If a typhoon was not looming he would have used this conflict to feed his habits; as it was, he stayed.

Samuel and Geraldine have been married twenty-six years. In the course of those twenty-six years Geraldine has run off to Samar, to her parent's home at least once a month. Samuel would wait a few days and then come fetch her. A typhoon may be forecast, but to Geraldine the budget was always on her mind, more alive and uncertain than any storm.

"Someday I hope for a bigger catch so we can fix this place up."

Samuel let this comment die. He had started fishing with his father as a young child, and together they put his brothers through school. He, the eldest, is the only uneducated one in the family. That Samuel knows the winds, the sea, the fishing and the boats, does not seem valuable. It does not seem valuable to him because that is not valued in his country. In some distorted twist of culture, a profession that demands the body and mind work together is despised and poorly compensated. So Samuel, like any tradesman, apologizes for his lack of education and income and then goes about his work of providing food and sustenance to a society which scorns him. This is his burden, one Geraldine shares, but cannot understand. That he gambles and drinks wine is his surrender.

Samuel and Geraldine finished their long drinking spree at 4:00 pm. Like all their drinking sprees it was flush with laughter and relaxation mixed with tension and anger.

It is routine when a typhoon, or tropical depression is approaching that the Coast Guard patrols the coastline and with loudspeakers instruct the fishermen not to leave the port. The "tough guys" often leave before the Coast Guard patrol boats arrive. They slip from their moorings hours before normal, the danger muted by their families' needs. It is too hard for fishermen to leave double prices in the sea. On the 7th of November, Thursday afternoon, with a super typhoon forecast, the Coast Guard never came. Either they just didn't care and were too busy with their own preparations, or they couldn't imagine fishermen would truly attempt to venture out. The 4:00 pm warning time came and went.

At 5:00 pm Samuel was on the shore with a few others. Imbit was there.

"No Coast Guard today?" Imbit asked. His boy was at his side. He was a thin boy with black hair and wide set eyes. His feet were broad and toes splayed from years of walking and working barefoot. He looked quietly at his father.

"Doesn't make sense," someone else said.

"Maybe the storm is just news, not real. There is no warning," Imbit said. "I may go out," he added and looked around.

Rene, another fisherman from the village shrugged his shoulders and said, "I have children. They have stomachs."

Someone laughed.

Imbit looked around him. The bay had a few ripples, the sky still light in the afternoon sun was mostly clear. His son, with the broad feet, was scraping the soil with his toes, his head was down. His son's clothes were worn, as were the bodies of his other children. Imbit didn't laugh, but his mind was settled. "Okay then," he said, "Let's catch some fish."

"You stay here though," he told his boy.

The two fishermen, Rene and Imbit, prepared their boats for fishing, settling their nets, lashing the loose bamboo outriggers, tying down their small canopies. Rene and Imbit are considered very "tough guys," two of the toughest. They are both built for fishing—thick bodied, heavy boned and strong as a carabao—but beyond that they are men who feed their families. For fishermen in Tacloban feeding families takes a trinity of toughness, combining daring, defiance and devotion.

Samuel watched them, the *tuba* still swimming in his veins. It was hard to stand on the shore with the villagers, the unspoken awe of his neighbors thick and fog-like in the air directed past him. He turned to his cousin and said, "They are just committing suicide." And then, as he strode back home, the wine hardened into regret about his decision not to fish...yet thankfulness too.

The news of the winds and direction of this storm troubled him.

It was on a direct path for Tacloban. He was afraid this was more than a signal two typhoon as some of the newscasts predicted. On the sea and in a typhoon's direct path, God alone knew what would happen. He tried not to put himself into a place where God was needed. He looked at the sky and felt the wind that was still blowing gently. It was a *Kanaway* wind. He did not think of God often, but he thought of Him now.

It must be so different from those who live here, who grew up here and who suffered here. Yesterday on the plane, a mother holding tight her child panicked when the plane entered the clouds and was being buffeted by the turbulence. "What is happening?" she cried. My wife held her hand and the mother buried her head into the seat. She was in front of us and only her eyes could be seen peering back at us, wild and afraid, like a trapped animal. She was coming home to Tacloban. Last night when the city creaked and groaned like an old barn I am sure she quivered and cried in her remembrance.

—From an aid worker's journal, 2014, Tacloban, Philippines

C H A P T E R   1

An Uncertain Calm

N O E L   L I T O

Noel Lito woke up at 6:00 am, November 7, the day before Typhoon Yolanda. A line was gathering at the single latrine in the corner of his cell. There were forty-three men crammed into this tiny room. They shared a single toilet. There was a rule for the latrine. There were rules for everything and they were strictly enforced with beatings. When Noel was first assigned to this cell he made three mistakes. The first time he forgot to bring the pail out of the CR (bathroom) and he'd received five blows. The second time he had fallen asleep when he had been asked to stand guard and suffered fifteen blows and the third time he had fought with another inmate over cooking wood and he had been hit twenty-five times. Each time he had to lie spread-eagled and face down on the concrete floor.

Each cell has its *berdugo*, the punisher. That is his name and his job. Noel remembered each beating from his *berdugo*, each brutal stoke on his naked back. He remembered the rough concrete on his belly and loins, the hands holding his feet and hands. The beatings seemed like yesterday. Noel lay in his bunk, careful not to look at anything.

Noel was twenty-two years old, the youngest incarcerated in

this cell by almost four years. Each of the twenty-seven cells in the Tacloban City Jail was sub-divided by age group and sex. His cell housed twenty-five to twenty-nine year old men. He had been in the Tacloban City Jail for five years and three months. He had yet to have a trial, yet to have a hearing.

Noel was seventeen years old when he had been arrested and charged with robbery and violence against a woman. He and two friends robbed a girl of her cell phone. One of the boys had carried a knife. Before he was apprehended Noel had prepared for prison life. It may seem odd that a seventeen-year-old would know anything about prison preparation, but Noel was a desperately poor male in the Philippines. He was immersed in a community of beaten down homeless people. He lived with neighbors who had survived decades of substandard living and subjection to a few powerful elites and their political cronies. Noel had expected to be apprehended. It was impossible to keep secrets in his community. Stories were circulating and people were being paid off. The girl they had robbed was from a prominent family. He was too young to think about transferring or running.

There are two gangs in the Tacloban City jail, the BSL's (Batang Samar Leyte Gang) and the BCD's (Batang City Jail). It was not an option for Noel to join or not to join. Convicts, or soon to be convicts, as in Noel's case, are visited by an agent from each gang and pressured to join one band or the other. The alternative is to become a prison slave of all the inmates. Noel joined the Batang Samar Leyte Gang, which permanently initiated him into their lawless cartel.

It had been a year since Noel's case was last before the Judge. It was always being postponed. When his case files were read in court the Judge would ask for a motion and his court appointed lawyer, Attorney Makila, would be busy with something, fiddling with papers, organizing a folder. The request for a motion would hang in the air. Noel would wait silently in his shackles. The Judge would suspend his case. Noel would shuffle back to his cell.

When Noel had been in jail for four years his court appointed attorney, Attorney Makila, had received a new appointment. He became a Judge in Carigara, Leyte, one of the original trial courts. Noel did not know who his new court appointed lawyer was, or if he even had one. If convicted he would serve four years, but four years had long passed. Jun Fajardo, one of his cellmates, had been here for twelve years and had yet to have a hearing.

Noel lay quietly in his bunk and rubbed one of his many tattoos. He had a lot of tattoos with names on them. There was Tony Alegro on his right shoulder, a bluish black skull with a square nose, wide eyes and curling eyebrows. Andy Warz in red and greens decorated his right thigh. Char lit up his left thigh and into his groin with bright orange flames. Jupiter Cuizon was splayed across his back. He had too many tattoos, too many names. In prison—unlike the outside or perhaps just like the outside, but different—excessive tattoos meant you were secondhand. He had been used. There was no doubt of that. It was why he had his own bunk, while the majority slept on the floor, or four together. It was why he was twenty-two and his cellmates twenty-five and older. But Noel was a fatalist like many Filipinos, taking the worst that men could give, resigned to his situation, almost content that evil was survivable.

He crawled out of his bunk and took his place in the latrine line. His place was near the front and based on position and rank. He took his "cuts" as expected and no one said a word. There was a rule that if a man could not wait to urinate he was allowed to ask politely to take cuts and it was another rule that you must allow him to move ahead. One of the prisoners by the name of Mark was in charge of the latrine line. It was well known that Mark had been named, not for St. Mark, but for the mark on his leg. He had been born with a red baseball-sized birthmark. They called him the "marked man", but never to his face. Mark was sensitive. Mark watched the line this morning and there were no issues. There rarely were.

Noel waited patiently as each man urinated in turn. No one spoke. No one laughed. The window to his cell faced north. The bars shadowed the sun that filtered in. The sunny courtyard beckoned. It was a warm and beautiful day. Noel thought about his guitar and his composition, "Four Kinds of Love." He could not wait to play it.

Breakfast was a silent affair. Jokes, coughs and sneezes were not allowed during meals. Noel stood in place and waited for his food. He could not ask for food or ask for seconds or ask a fellow inmate to share. He must wait to be served. Once seated he was not allowed to transfer to another location. All these were punishable offenses and *berdugo* was always watching. These rules made sense to Noel, sense that had come with beatings. He understood that prisoners are sensitive to change and even laughter would cause conflict. Anything to stop conflict was good for him. Forty-three men in a twenty-five square meter room lined with bunks is not a place for conflict. So Noel waited and was served and sat quietly eating his two slices of *tinapay* bread, drinking coffee and thinking about his day.

There was no routine after breakfast. The men were let out of their cells to hang out in the common courtyard. Noel spent his time roaming around and strumming his guitar. He tried to feel the mood of the day, not the weather so much as the emotions that were being played out among the other convicts, the always present tension of men bunched together like lobsters in a holding tank, their claws barely tied. Roaming was his protection. He felt like he was on the run, running from trouble, but it was very careful running. He was careful to look like he was not running, just wandering aimlessly. After five years there was nothing aimless in Noel's travels Thursday morning or any other day. He was always adjusting to the ebb and flow of prison emotion. It was not second nature or unconscious action. It was a deliberate and intentional keenness honed to keep him alive and safe.

For a few hours he found peace in a courtyard corner playing his guitar and working on his latest song "Four Kinds of Love." He had a rich even voice and he sang softly over and over:

Four kinds of love
One childhood love
Two-puppy love
And three stupid loves

Sometimes it is hard to fall in love
Even if you stay away it will be hard
Even if you've given it all it is not enough

He thought about his wife Maricris, whom he had married two years earlier. He had been introduced to her through some friends. The romance had blossomed through the technical advances and cheapness of the text. Their marriage had been sanctified and sealed in the "coffins"—they were coffins in size only, room enough for two to lie in visible privacy—provided for the conjugal visits. Noel sang and thought about Maricris, imagining their visits in the coffins and the life recently conceived in its dark and stifling interior. He had a child coming; this was foremost on his mind.

During the Thursday morning head count, Noel was given two eight-ounce cans of sardines for his meals on Friday and Saturday. He was told this was in preparation for the coming super typhoon. He felt this was a small bonus and tucked his sardines away in the rafters along with a stash of rice and a few of his other belongings. The coming super typhoon was the least of Noel's worries. He was happy for the two cans of sardines.

Noel played his guitar and roamed around for an hour. The prisoners all have a routine and this was his. It was simple. It was careful. He was okay with it.

It rained all night. Poured all night. Our room on the second floor under a roof that does not leak was comforting. Like the wind of the first night, the pounding rain of this night brought back fond memories of water on tin, the steady drum, the crescendos of the tropical storm rising and falling and I a gentle bystander in the audience enjoying the orchestra, sleeping when I want to sleep and listening when I want to listen, but all the while I must remember those outside, not in the audience, those who cannot hear the music, only feel the pounding wetness and the reverberating cold.

—From an aid worker's journal, 2014, Tacloban, Philippines

C H A P T E R   1

An Uncertain Calm

A L L A N   L A B I T A

On Thursday, November 7, 2013, Allan Labita rose at 6:00 am to prepare breakfast for his family. He pulled out some leftovers, made some coffee and watched the morning light seep in from an overhead crack. It was a sunny day. The wind was light and balmy. The sky was clear. There was no sign of a coming storm. Normally with a typhoon approaching there would be rain falling and the sky would be dark and threatening. To Allan this looked like another beautiful day, a kite-flying day.

Allan spent a few minutes in the bathroom before the family rose. He rinsed his black hair. A threadbare mustache and chin beard thins out his face. His eyes are heavy and dark and his skin swarthy. He looked in the mirror at his teeth slightly crooked and his smile offset. He took a moment to tie his beard with a rubber band, twisting it slightly and stroking it pencil lead thin with his thumb and forefinger. He pushed back his hair, thinking about his beautiful wife Dana, not yet home from her twelve-hour night shift, wondering if she would go to work this evening—the super typhoon on his mind—or perhaps she would have the night off with him.

Breakfast was pizza. Fourteen lived in this home in Barangay 83, in the San Jose District. Allan's mother was the second one up. "Coffee is on Mom."

"Okay, where are my *tinapay* rolls?" Allan's mother always had coffee and breakfast rolls. This was her routine and it stretched back to Allan's earliest memories.

"By your chair mom."

Allan's three brothers, Arnel, Kim, and Arman, took their turn in the bathroom and congregated in the kitchen, drinking coffee and eating cold pizza.

"How is the weather? Arman asked.

"Sunny," said Allan. "I did not expect it to be sunny today."

Aileen got up with her two-year-old daughter baby Coleen.

"Come to Uncle Kim." Coleen was a favorite of Kim's and he spent hours with her babysitting and playing. She went willingly.

"Franco wants me to evacuate," said Aileen. Aileen's husband Franco was a merchant marine currently stationed in the Baltic Sea near Poland.

"Really, are you going to?" asked Allan.

"I don't think so. I would rather be here with the family."

"It is up to you; everyone should do what they think is right."

"When did you hear from him?" asked Kim.

"Yesterday on Facebook," Aileen replied. "He is worried from the reports."

"It's a super typhoon," yelled Armida, another sister, from the second bedroom.

"If he was here I would go." It was hard for Eileen. Franco was not in Tacloban. He couldn't smell the air, feel the easy breeze and shady heat. He couldn't sip on coffee with the family as they started another day in the tropics. He was a member of the family, but an absent member. It was not the same.

"I am home." Dana, Allan's wife, called from the front door. She had just finished her night shift as a caregiver.

"How was work?" Allan asked.

"Okay," she said.

Allan wanted to greet her with a hug or a kiss, but there was no privacy. Allan and Dana did not believe in public affection, and their home was a public place. They shared a look. That was all.

"Do you want a coffee?"

"No, I will shower first. Are the kids awake?" Allan and Dana's children, Phill, Ax, Yugi and Bridgette were lounging in their room.

"Not yet, no school today."

"How are they?"

"Good."

"Phill, their oldest was standing at the bedroom door. He had been listening to the conversations.

"I wonder if the typhoon will break the house?" he asked.

"Probably," Allan replied.

"We will pray to God it doesn't," Dana said.

Mother just grunted from the lazy chair.

"If it does we can build a better one. One just for us," Allan said, looking at Dana.

"That's a dream," she answered.

"Yeah, that's true. Hey Phill, look at what the kite angel did!" Phill's kite, broken from yesterday's flight, was hanging from a nail on the wall. The torn wings had been magically repaired.

Between talk and pizza, Tina, Allan's third sister getting up and preparing for work; Dana cleaning up after her night shift, dishes, mother with her prayers, the children getting dressed—the day began.

Allan's mother's ancestral home is a small three-room house with extensions. It was marginally built of hollow blocks with scabbed-on wooden lean-tos. It has a galvanized shed roof on a coconut lumber frame. The house has been under construction for years. The entryway is half-done. Bouquets of rusty re-rod protrude from the tops of the exterior walls. There are no interior doors. The comfort room, the single bedroom and the two lean-tos are protected with privacy blankets. It is a comfortable home for four, but with nine adults and five children only mother in her easy chair has a place of her own. Allan and Dana share a room with their four children and ten listening ears.

Allan stepped outside and breathed the sea air, the ocean a kilometer away. The Labita family home sits ten meters off the street and is ringed by neighbors whose walls attach to their walls. A narrow concrete walk with a wall on the left side and a fence on the right lead into their tiny residence. The walk is clean and neat, with orchids hanging on each side, spilling over their vases and adorning the path with their petals.

In communities such as Allan's, bundled together like sheaves of a newspaper, when someone steps outside they are immersed in a disheveled neighborhood of different ideas and personalities. Allan's purpose Thursday morning was to find coherence in the differing news reports on the coming typhoon. Conversations were being shared on every corner, at every gate and each walkway. At the *sari-sari* stores the men were gathered, talking.

Allan and his brother Kim made their way to another gathering place, the Rimas, a huge towering breadfruit tree, a few prickly fruits hanging. It was well over four hundred years old. One neighbor looked at its thick trunk and branches and said, "Maybe Yolanda will be so pretty it will knock this tree down." It was a sarcastic comment, a "pretty" storm. But this was the community consensus Thursday morning. This is what the men and women in Allan's neighborhood worked out as they studied the news and mixed it in with their long history of typhoons and storms and life in the San Jose District. The Typhoon was big; they knew that. But the Rimas tree had stood the tests of thousands of typhoons and it still bore fruit and still gave shade. Their neighborhood was a tropical paradise of coconut palms, mahogany trees and the occasional breadfruit tree. It was filled with homes built of concrete and re-rod. Some were large, such as the counselors three-story mansion across the alley from Allan's home. Most of the houses were lifetime construction projects, small concrete homes with appendages to accommodate growing families. Allan's barrio had little space left to build or add on and the zero-property lines gave the feeling of one large sprawling building. In its mass and shifting life it seemed a powerful immovable force, a force the ocean a kilometer away could not destroy.

"Oh, this tree will be around when we are long gone," Allan replied.

"Are you evacuating to the Astrodome?" the neighbor Tata Leo asked. The Tacloban arena is a seven-thousand seat round covered stadium referred to by everyone as the "Astrodome."

"No, not us. But we are preparing. There is a storm surge they say, fifteen-foot storm surge. It is just a big wave. It will never reach us. We need to worry about the wind and rain."

"Yeah, we aren't leaving either. George did that last year."

They all knew about George. He was a neighbor who had evacuated to the Astrodome in 2012 when a super typhoon had been predicted. His home had been looted.

"You would have to drag George away this year," Kim answered.

Daniel sauntered over to the Rimas tree. He was a short squat man who made fish balls and sold them in the market. His day normally started at 3:00 am, meeting the first of the fishermen delivering their catch at the Tacloban market, continuing over an open fire and long hours behind a fish stand. With the storm coming he was taking the day off. "They keep talking about a storm surge, but what the hell is that?" he asked.

"Just a strong storm," someone said.

"It is a rising of the water. The wind is pushing it." Allan understood the English word "surge," which few in his neighborhood did, but he did not consider it a tsunami. He had no way to reference the word surge in his dialect or in his history and no media or government was providing that reference.

"Typhoons here, typhoons there. We are survivors," said Daniel.

"I suppose this tree will go nowhere. The roots of the Rimas tree are under all our houses."

"I am not taking this storm lightly," said Allan. "They are saying it is a category five. We have never seen a category five."

"Look at Uncle Alex." Allan's brother Kim interrupted.

They all looked at Uncle Alex play with the kids. He was running down the street in his sandals and baggy shorts, his hair uncombed, his belly round and bouncing, trying to get a kite in the air.

There was concern in the community, a bustle of preparation, but also a holiday feel. Everything was closed, or if still open, filled with talk of closing. The city government of Tacloban had declared a "no-work day," and only those who were part of the city's contingency plan were allowed to report to their offices. Uncle Alex, who lived next door, worked for the city. He had the day off and he was unconcerned, laughing in the street with the neighborhood children, doing his best to launch kites into the sky.

The day before the typhoon was a kite-flying day, which was unusual in itself. There was no rain, at least not yet. The light breeze was perfect. Each of Allan's children had a handmade kite, made from tiny barbeque sticks fit into a cross and covered with plastic bags cut out like diamonds. The barbeque sticks are stitched together with fish line, finely and firmly wound. A tail hangs from the diamond for stability and two small wings on each side are attached for balance. Kites are a small gift Allan keeps giving to his children—a day of flying and the kites are invariably damaged—in the evenings when the children are sleeping he rebuilds them, repairing the broken limbs, replacing the torn shells and sorting out the twisted string. Allan's kites are bigger than the average, two feet by two feet. The repair that happens miraculously each night is part of their beauty. It makes miraculous seem possible and maybe because of this the kids love to fly kites as much for this miracle as for the reality.

Allan has encouraged his children to build their imagination and hope from outside of their daily lives. He has allowed his children to question everything around them, even himself, which his mother and his wife find borderline disrespectful, but he thinks this will help his children overcome the Filipino syndrome of inferiority; the class system pressed on him and his family by economic oppression and historical conquest.

He encourages his children to dream because he dreams himself.

It allows him to live in quiet and constant rebellion against the status quo of being poor and being poorly treated.

Allan and the men and woman of the neighborhood prepared for a typhoon, something they do many times in the course of their year— there were papers to store in plastic bags, water to bottle, food to pack, medical kits to check, personal items and clothes to gather, roofs to tie down, prayers to say and saints to put up—all the while the children flew kites on the street, the light plastic bags dipping and weaving in the wind, the boys leaping over obstacles while tugging and freeing and doing their utmost to keep aloft a fragile bird on a string.

I walk the shore between two worlds. The world of destroyed man and the world of an endless God. I look to see what I can find in the destroyed world of man. I pick away at the debris and scuff sand away. I pick up things and see if they have value. I have even carried things for a while, until I was tired of their weight. And I look at the endless world of God, the sky always changing, and always alive. The sea and the breakers flowing in and in and in. The white foam, the changing sand.

—From an aid worker's journal, 2014, Tacloban, Philippines

CHAPTER 1

An Uncertain Calm

DOLOR LINGO

Dolor Lingo turned thirty-six years old on November 7, the day before Yolanda hit Tacloban. She and her husband Dante lived in Barangay 89, San Jose, which is still in Tacloban, but bordering the Municipality of Palo. They have four children: thirteen-year-old Daniel, twelve-year-old Dante Jr., seven-year-old David Carl, and five-year-old Princess Diana their only girl.

Dolor has a wide face, with wide eyes, her long hair shadows clear features. She looks her age but that is not a bad thing. Everything about her is open and honest. She is not heavy and not thin, one of those people who work and live and die healthy, if that is possible.

Dante, a year younger than Dolor, is more serious, more unquestioning. For years an American missionary has mentored him. It has given him a foundation to build on, a purpose and a belief on which to stand. But as a young Filipino, guided by an older American, the relationship is vertical. There is he, Dante, above him is the American missionary and then there is God. In Dante's land there is a cultural subjection to the west, stretching back four hundred years to Spain's religious rule and followed by fifty years of American governance. General MacArthur's monument—representing the World War II return and liberation in Palo is just two kilometers from the Lingo's home—Dante drives by it daily. MacArthur's father was the third governor of the Philippines in 1900 and he along with other Americans brought education and in their education they became the teacher and the Filipino became the student.

Dante is still a student. The American identity and his Filipino identity have not yet merged into his own person.

At 7:00 am Dolor and Dante discussed the coming typhoon. They were drinking coffee.

"Did you hear about the typhoon?" asked Dante.

"Yes, I heard about it from Theresa," she was a neighbor.

"What do you think?"

"Just a typhoon. We get them every year."

"This seems like a big one."

"God will protect us."

"Your sister is going around telling everyone to evacuate." Dolor's sister, Nanita, was a barangay official.

Dolor and Dante's home is seventy-five yards from the San Pedro Bay. They built their house themselves from scraps of metal and wood. The rafters and stud walls are coconut lumber, a "celery wood," having a tough stalk and an airy core, which is not a structural wood, but it's cheap and available.

"That is just her job. She and her kids are staying at mother's tonight. Anyway we are safe here. God is in control," said Dolor.

Dante had to agree with that. He couldn't argue with God. The truth was neither of them were overly concerned. They experienced numerous typhoons each year and were confident their house would protect them, because it was strongly nestled in among other homes and butted up against the massive Hot Chile Factory, with its deep rows of cement vaults unused for the last fifteen years. In past typhoons, their oil lamps—buried as their house was among these concrete structures—would not flicker.

Dolor and Dante had a full day before them. The rice bin was almost empty and Dante needed some morning transactions to fill it up again. Dante is a scrap dealer, which means he goes around the neighborhood looking and buying—much like people buy scrap everywhere in the world. He buys from one person and sells it a little higher to someone else on the scrap chain. Dante is also an assistant pastor and worship leader at his church. But for livelihood he is a scrap dealer. When he and Dolor first married, he started collecting garbage on his way back and forth from the bible school he was attending. He turned it into a walking scrap business. Back then he and Dolor had prayed to God for a vehicle and sure enough they acquired an old bicycle. The bicycle allowed him to carry more scrap, so he asked the Lord for a pedicab. The business grew and he prayed for a motorcycle. He had borrowed money from a *bumbay* (illegal money lender) to buy the motorcycle. That God's provision would come in this questionable way was not something he questioned.

Dolor is a business owner. She also calls herself a "personal shopper" or the manager of a "pre-need" company. The neighborhood definition of her business is pre-need. Pay now, order and get later. Her business is like Amway but called Boardwalk. She takes orders for such things as perfume, pants and shoes. Dolor's boardwalk business is like many other international marketing companies embedded in her community.

At 9:00 am on Thursday there was a light rain. School was cancelled. Princess Diana and David Carl were playing in the house. Daniel and Dante Jr. had run to their Grandma's to watch TV. Dante was out collecting metals. Dolor was texting orders on her cell phone. The day was ordinary and the Lingo family did ordinary things. They worked as they worked every other day. They ate what little they had. Their children played as children should play, creatively. They gave thanks for everything.

At 2:00 pm Dante came home from his rounds. He unloaded the scrap he had bought, storing it at the house for sale after the storm.

"Dolor, I think we should think about evacuating." Dante had met with his American mentor and was worried.

"Oh?" She was still figuring her orders.

"I was told the Tacloban Plaza Hotel has some vacancies."

"How much will that cost?"

"Fifteen hundred."

Dolor did not respond immediately. They both knew they did not have fifteen hundred pesos. "Do you want some rice?"

"Sure." Dante had not eaten.

"I am not worried about the typhoon. We'll be fine." Dolor served some rice from the rice pot, still warm from the noon meal.

"I was just thinking it might be a wise move."

"We still have two debts. We owe our neighbors four hundred pesos for the rice you are eating. How can we pay for a hotel?"

In the Philippines borrowing from neighbors is part of survival. If Dolor cannot borrow from a neighbor, she will be stuck borrowing from the "five/sixers" or "*bumbays*" as they are called, a name based on their common nationality, people who lend at rates exceeding two hundred percent. This is how Dante had financed his motorcycle. Or a borrower will have to seek out one of the many "non-profits" who find a way to be money-lenders—at interest rates between twenty-five and one hundred percent—and not profitable at the same time. This is the option Dolor and Dante have as members of poor Filipino society, to borrow from neighbors as needy as themselves or to borrow from cutthroat lenders. Lenders who come riding their motorcycles in their wolves clothing or lenders setting up their non-government organizations cloaked with various kinds of sheeply garb. Both take, neither ultimately give.

"Maybe we should send the kids over to mother's," said Dolor. "A lot of the family are going there and it will be fun for them."

"Okay," said Dante, for this was their only option.

Dolor's mother's home was recently renovated. It had a solid cement foundation, reinforced pillars, hollow-block walls, a heavy gauge tin roof and rafters constructed of the old lumber, dry, dark brown and hard as nails. It was forty yards from the open sea on a narrow ocean road that wound along a black sandy shore lined with coconut palms and sea grass. It was less than twenty meters from Dolor and Dante's home but separated by three other homes. It was a central gathering spot for her extended family.

"I will get the house ready then." Dante went outside to prepare for what was coming.

"I will be inside. Call me when you need me."

Dolor busied herself with chores. Dante went about the job of securing their roof. He gathered the hollow blocks and rope he needed.

Dolor came outside when the light rain had stopped. It was partly sunny. The temperature hovered around 30 degrees Celsius. Dante was on the roof. She handed him some blocks.

"I need more."

"That should be enough."

"No I think I need more. Do we have more rope?"

"I do, but I don't think you need it."

"Yes, I want to be sure."

Dante kept asking for more, more rope, more blocks. They worked for two hours and she kept telling him he had done enough, the roof was fine, but he was not sure. Dolor was sure. Her sister Nanita, the barangay official, may be instructing people to evacuate to the Astrodome, the massive covered stadium on the bay in Tacloban, but it was not necessary. Nanita was not encouraging Dolor to evacuate and she was not evacuating herself.

Dolor went back to her daily chores. Dante continued to work securing their home. The children were playing at her mother's house by the bay. A few of the neighbors were moving to shelters set up in the city. The sun was intermittent and there was an occasional threat of rain, but not enough to stop Dolor from hanging the clothes.

She hummed to herself as she worked, a beautiful old hymn, *It is Well With My Soul,* taught to her by American missionaries from Tennessee. The words "when sorrows like sea billows roll" drifted gently in the breeze.

This precarious walk between two worlds, one of single sandals, paint brushes with no brushes, soggy animals, broken glass, torn clothes, rusted electronics and the other world, the one of sea and sand and sky are the story of my life, but not so distinct. These walks I have taken on Tacloban beach are walks of reflection, they can be nothing else. This is a boardwalk of life in all its ugly distinction. I am curious about the one and I love the other. I question men and wonder at God. How is it we man invest in such temporal things? The list of broken and destroyed items goes on and on. They are made from the same elements God had made, yet they are trinkets and unless we preserve them in some tomb or conditioned structure they will rot, fade and corrode to nothing.
—From an aid worker's journal, 2014, Tacloban, Philippines

C H A P T E R   1

An Uncertain Calm

C A R L I T O   Q U I A S

Thursday, November 7, the day before Typhoon Yolanda was projected to hit Tacloban, Carlito Quias got up at his usual time of 4:00 am. He strolled out of his hollow block home situated fifty meters from the ocean, pulled out a cigarette, lit it and looked at the stars sharp and clear in the sky. He had lived here for fifteen years and this was his routine, step out into the quiet of the early morning, enjoy a smoke before his breakfast of coffee and bread. The early morning sky signaled another beautiful day. He was surprised by the clear stillness. For the last week there had been rumors about a super typhoon and he expected to see rain clouds, cooler temperatures and wind.

He fingered his cigarette, cupping his hands around the flame, which did not flutter. He was sixty years old, thin, wizened from years of sun and hard labor. He wore a ball cap and bifocal prescription glasses that had cost him over one thousand pesos. His glasses, his cigarettes, his ball cap, a quiet walk in the morning gazing at the sky and listening to the ocean were enough for him. He had worked hard in his life, but now as the owner of eight pedicabs—seven that he rented out daily to other drivers—the husband of a hard-working wife and a home full of his third wife's children and grandchildren, he was content.

Carlito's life had started quickly. His mother had died when he was six. He was more or less orphaned at fourteen, when his father stabbed a neighbor during an escalating argument. Actually he didn't just stab a neighbor; he stabbed the man until dead.

They lived in Samar at the time. His father ended up in the hospital with a serious head wound. Upon recovery he was transferred to a small holding cell in the Balugo Carridad, Salcedo. He could have paid the other family money, but he chose to go to jail, figuring the family would kill him anyway. He was transferred to the Muntinlupa jail in Manila upon conviction.

Carlito and his siblings drifted their own way after the murder. At the age of sixteen he married his first wife, Linda. They moved to greater Manila and he went to work in a garment factory in Cainta, Rizal, owned by a Korean family by the name of Choy. He was paid six pesos for an eight-hour day. Forty-seven years ago it was not a legal job. School was never an option.

He and Linda left Manila and returned to Samar, where he fathered two children. When he was eighteen Linda wanted to visit her family in Calobia, Leyte. Carlito took her there and within two weeks she had decided to relocate. He returned alone to Samar to get their belongings, but on the way changed his mind and moved to Taytay, Rizal, near Manila. Off and on Linda sent messages, but he had decided life was too hard in Calobia—the only jobs were working as a farmhand, planting rice, vegetables and root crops, jobs that enslaved a person with low pay and long hours—he never answered.

In Taytay he found a job with a construction company. In 1998 he married again, this time in a church, to Rosia Carabara who was working at another garment factory, also in Taytay.

Rosia wanted to move back to Samar, where she was from, to live with her parents. So they moved to Legaspi, Samar. He fathered three boys over the course of twelve years. The marriage was rife with mistrust and conflict. Again he left for Manila.

This "migration," from province to Manila and back again is part of being poor in the Philippines. The opportunity of the city beckons, but its grandeur fades with the reality of slums and squatter homes that are packed like crates on every available piece of earth. The jobs are temporary, the living conditions harsh and then the lush countryside and family homes beckon and back and forth the people go, until they end in one place or another, fatigued and hopeless, often with more than one family.

Eventually Carlito met another woman, Claring, in Manila and they married, but not really. They just lived together. This has become marriage for many in the Philippines. The poor are caught between an inability to pay the church, the government, and the government's corrupt officials—who may be more desperate than corrupt —so they do the next best thing. They marry without the politics and church and for the most part the culture they live in is okay with this. They are accepted as married. All around them families are in similar situations of cohabitation, but the families would never profess that. They profess only that they are married. It is one of the dynamics of being poor in a Catholic society where biology trumps a societal rule. In their hearts they do the best they can to accommodate the two. The church does not make this easy. It does not recognize them as married. It does not allow them to take communion. On occasion mass ceremonies take place to placate the church's sense of propriety, but for the most part life goes on and cohabitation becomes even more an accepted norm.

The Thursday before Typhoon Yolanda as Carlito looked out through his bifocals, the stars shined back at him and hid any thoughts he might have about his first two children, his other two wives, and the brothers and sisters he had not seen for years. Those people were gone and forgotten, like the shell of a coconut or the peel of a banana, long discarded. Carlito thought about his day. He thought about his pedicabs. He thought about the four hundred pesos he would make on them. He thought about collecting yesterday's earnings. He thought about the tin of cash he had hidden and he thought about Claring, whom he had married fifteen years before. She was a hard woman, but he was content.

Carlito ate his bread and coffee, grabbed his ball cap, cigarettes, and unchained his pedicab. His pedicab, like all pedicabs, are bicycles with a covered frame and a bench seat welded to the side. There are no multi-gear sprockets, nothing to make the cycling easy. The Philippines are full of Sunday bikers, riding in packs or solo, using the latest bikes, and bike clothes and helmets and shoes. But the country is also full of pedicab drivers, those who bike with loaded carts for hours on end. Unlike the weekend wheelers, the pedicab tires are never spinning, their wheels struggle over the ruts and up the gradients, making slow and tortuous progress.

At sixty Carlito is full of sinews and hardened muscles, with a thin layer of skin, like clear grease, that makes these muscles undulate like rocks in clear water. This is the kind of body the Sunday bikers would like to have, but no one looks at Carlito and sees anything but an old man on a pedicab, a poor man who struggles down the side streets, or waits at the schools, or hauls lumber from the lumber yards.

Thursday morning Carlito started out on Baybay road and made his way to the DZR Airport road. A pedicab driver drives around like a taxi driver looking for people to pick up and Carlito spent his morning doing this, as he had done for the last fifteen years. He picked up a few people at the nearby jeepney stop coming home from their night shift. He pedaled his way down various residential streets delivering passengers, picking up others, making eight to ten pesos at a time. Occasionally someone would talk about the typhoon, but for the most part people just hung on to their bags or purses and sat quietly on the shared bench seat.

At 12:00 pm, Carlito's work day was complete. His morning had been slow. Many of the government workers had been given the day off, but he had made a few extra pesos. Claring was also home, done with her shift at the Bay View Inn where she had worked for fifteen years, washing bed sheets, cleaning rooms. In fact everyone was home because of the coming typhoon. Gathered at the house were four of Claring's six children (Jun, Edwin, Roning, Friggy), and six of their grandchildren (Cyron, Sandro, Jennymae, Jenelyn, baby Sunshine and baby Girl), her daughter-in-law Elna, Clarito's youngest son Rex from his second marriage, and Rex's pregnant wife Reah, who lived next door.

The family ate their standard lunch, which consisted of sardines, *tuyo* (smoked fish) and rice. The grandkids were running around in excitement. The adults ate and listened to the radio. They heard the English words "storm surge" the radio announcers kept repeating, but they did not understand them. All of them spoke Waray and some broken English. There was no translation of storm surge, so they assumed it meant a strong storm which they had lived through many times before.

The un-tombing of Tacloban. The stripping away of all we hold precious, leaves only what is truly precious, which is life in its most elemental form. The land, the sea, the sky and the child playing among it all.
—From an aid worker's journal, 2014, Tacloban, Philippines

CHAPTER 1

An Uncertain Calm

REGIE PAA

On November 7, Regie Paa was sleeping in the stuffy interior of a Toyota Crosswind van. He had left the windows open to allow some ventilation. Insects had filled the interior. Sleeping in a hot van—even the most comfortable one in the lot—surrounded by pavement and twenty-four hour traffic was a far cry from the cool sea breeze and thickly oxygenated air of his province.

He woke up slowly, the tinted windows obscured the sun that had risen forty minutes earlier at 6:00 am. Regie slept in the front seat, which was reclined back as far as it would go. He had a thin blanket and slept on his side. At twenty-nine years old he could still sleep curled up in a seat and wake up without his joints stiff and sore.

He stretched and looked out the window. There was no sign of the super typhoon that was being forecast. That was a good thing. His wife Bhe and his two children lived in Biliran, a distant one hundred and ten kilometers west, but also in the typhoon's path. Regie lived and worked at The Sto. Niño Car Mall located across from the Coke plant on a large roundabout. The Coke plant is two hundred meters from Cancabato Bay, just south of Tacloban City proper.

Regie has short dark hair, a slight build, but he is wiry and stronger than he looks. His eyes have a tendency to hold someone's attention and give attention at the same time. They are kind eyes, trustworthy eyes, good eyes for sales.

Regie is from Biliran. He was born and raised just off Bagacay Road, a winding mountainous trail notorious for thieves. To get to his family compound one has to follow a steep unmarked footpath, hidden to all but the most observant, or those who have lived in these villages. The path originates on one of Bagacay's hairpin turns which wrap around steep craggy banks. It starts on the top of the bank and disappears into the foliage of a tropical forest. If one finds it and follows it, the path reappears in the mountainous jungle, beaten down and broad. Flowers line the way and hollowed out stumps act as vases. Simple homes are scattered among the trees and the hillside. There are chickens, pigs, gardens, aunts, uncles and cousins.

Regie, his wife Bhe and their children, two-year-old Naphanien and six-year-old Hannah, own one of these simple homes, where water flows from a mountain stream far above them and gas lamps light their evenings. This is Regie and Bhe's home, but they rarely stay there. He has a college degree in mechanical engineering, which gives him this job as a car salesman in Tacloban. She is a certified teacher and works as a substitute teacher whenever she can. She is currently employed at the Core Elementary School in San Roque. Regie's mother cares for the children.

Regie is a mechanical engineering graduate, but anyone with a "good job" (above 200 pesos a day and no manual labor) in the Philippines has a college degree. To work at a supermarket as a cashier, to pour coffee in a coffee shop, to sell cars in a used car lot, these are college jobs.

Regie slapped at the mosquitoes that had filled the van. His associate Wendell was sleeping in the car next to him. Wendell loved to sleep. Regie slipped out the door and crept over to Wendell's car. He pounded on the window and then ducked out of sight.

Nothing.

He did it again, pounding on the window and ducking.

He saw a hand wave.

This was Regie's routine, a morning peek-a-boo with Wendell. They were both far from home, far from family, about the same age and good companions.

"Wendell, wake up, let's go to the canteen."

"No thanks, do not disturb me." Wendell always said that.

"Pal wake up. I'm hungry."

"Okay, okay."

They sauntered over to the canteen twenty meters from the car lot. They both ordered two cups of rice and *pakbet* (a vegetable dish which is a combination of squash and okra, eggplant, moringa or malunggay leaves, ginger and garlic). They drank water, which was free.

"No sign of the typhoon," said Wendell.

"If it comes we will just stay here anyway," replied Regie.

"Let's play some cards."

"Okay, I will do the cars, you get the crackers." Regie and Wendell play *tong-its*—a card game based on poker hands—and whoever wins eats a cracker. Regie headed to the car lot, Wendell went to the *sari-sari* store for some Oishi flavored crackers, their favorite.

Regie is the manager, security guard, secretary, driver, salesman, service man and appraiser all in one. He had worked and lived at this car mall for three years. Every three or four months he would make the one-hundred and ten kilometer trip to Biliran to see Bhe, the kids, his mother, father, aunts and uncles. His wife Bhe was working twenty-five kilometers from their mountainous enclave, so she too stayed away for weeks at a time. Regie and Bhe's choice was simple. They could pay bus fare and visit home, or send the money to buy rice and milk for the children. They chose the latter and lived with this arrangement.

The car mall works on an age-old method of dealership and deception. Regie appraises a car that comes in. He then calls his boss in Cebu, who negotiates the price that can be paid. Back and forth Regie will go with the owner of the car and his boss on the phone, until an agreement is reached. His boss then wires the money to the local Western Union. Regie picks up and delivers the cash and completes the transaction. The new old car is then sent to Cebu to the men with the magic hands. The men with the magic hands roll back the mileage from two hundred thousand to fifty or sixty thousand. They put in some additives and polish the engine and wheels. They add a basket rack, a rain visor. They Armor All the dash, covering the smells of human usage. They wrap the steering wheel with a "genuine" leather cover. They turn the newly-purchased old car into a doctored, relatively new car. Regie eventually gets it back and his job is to keep it new until he sells it.

The idea that he is complicit to a fair amount of automobile trickery is something Regie puts out of his mind. His life has no dark plots or hidden secrets. His profit from the whole scheme is simply a chance to earn a meager wage and provide food for his family. If he allowed himself to dwell on the moral issues at stake he would put his job at risk, so he put these thoughts aside. And he assumes, sometimes correctly, that anyone buying a car would know the mileage is not accurate. If a buyer questions it, he does not lie, he simply shows them the odometer and states the obvious.

At 8:00 am Regie started his workday by servicing and cleaning the five cars in the lot. He started each car. He let each engine run five minutes. He cleaned each wheel. He polished the chrome and washed windows. He mopped off the roadside dirt. As with breakfast this was his routine. Wendell, meanwhile, had bought the crackers and was spending his time washing up. Wendell was fastidious about staying clean and looking good.

"For my wife." he liked to say, though he saw her less than Regie saw Bhe.

"You done?" Wendell called. He had the back of one of the cars open and was dealing the cards.

Regie picked up his cards. "You survive the mosquitoes?"

"Yeah, I'm a survivor. You?"

"I got eaten all night. I feel like I am half here, but," Regie laid down his cards. "I'm going to be bigger than you. Give me a cracker."

"Have you checked the TV?" asked Wendell.

"Yeah, it is on. The storm is coming and it is big."

"I wish I could go home," said Wendell. "I am worrying about my wife and child."

"Yeah....me too. You lose again. You don't know how to play."

"Just deal."

Regie and Wendell played cards and monitored the TV throughout the morning. The car lot had a cable TV connection and each hour they checked the latest report. Regie watched the satellite images being shown, the massive red eye and swirling white vapor. At noon he called his boss in Cebu, to let him know the storm was heading directly for Tacloban. He also saw it was on track to cross Biliran and his provincial home.

"Sir, this is Regie. We are watching the storm. It looks like it will hit my province?"

"You need to stay at the display center," said his boss. "Nobody leave."

"He just cares about the money." Wendell said, when Regie was off the phone.

"Yeah, and if we leave, the cars will drive off too."

Regie's wife Bhe texted, from the Core Elementary School in San Roque. "Hearing about typhoon."

"Watching it too," texted Regie.

"I am worrying about the children."

Regie wasn't sure how to answer this. He was worried too, but what could he do about it? "Have you texted Rachel?" Rachel was Regie's cousin, who lived on the family compound and was old enough to have a phone and young enough to know how to use it.

"No signal there."

"Okay."

"You need to come and get me." Bhe had sent her money home—something she did daily—by a courier. Regie also sends his money home on a regular basis, but he keeps one thousand pesos for emergencies. One thousand pesos would provide transportation for himself and Bhe, but it was with him, ninety-five kilometers from her.

"Can you borrow some?"

"I am the only one left. Everybody evacuated."

"I have to stay here. Boss requirement."

"Family is more important."

"Cars will get stolen if I leave."

"I don't care about cars."

"I can ask Boss again."

"This is a big typhoon!!!"

The typhoon concerned Regie. The large red eye on the TV was ominous, but he had a job and his boss had made the job clear. It wasn't the loss of business his boss was concerned about. Regie knew full well that abandoning the lot would leave it accessible to looters and car thieves. There was little use in calling his boss.

"My wife wants me to go home and to pick her up on the way." Regie told Wendell.

"I'd like to go home too."

"If we do the cars will be stolen."

"I know; we can't leave these damn cars."

"I don't know what to tell Bhe."

"Tell her you have to work."

"Yeah right. I tried that."

Regie spent the early afternoon walking around the lot, responding lamely to his wife through text and communicating with his boss in Cebu.

On the round-a-bout the traffic was light. Many of the businesses had shut down. Service vehicles were not running. Trucking companies had closed. The little red KIAs with Coke Insignia were parked neatly at the Coke plant across the way. Regie noted all this, as well as the weather, which was mild and partly sunny.

"Are you coming?" Bhe texted.

Regie called his boss in Cebu again. "Boss, this is Regie."

"Hey Regie."

"My wife is in San Roque. I need to go and get her so she can get home."

"Regie you cannot leave the lot. You know that."

"Yeah."

"Hang in there Regie. It's just a storm. You'll be okay."

"Yeah, okay." Regie hung up and Bhe texted again.

"Are you coming?"

"Still checking," but his answer did not send.

"I am out of load." Regie told Wendell. "I am going to the *sari-sari* store for load. Bhe is very angry. She wants me to come. Boss wants us to stay. I am not sure what to do?"

"Are you coming?" Bhe texted again.

Regie walked to the store a few hundred meters away. He bought 100 pesos of load and waited for it to activate. It didn't activate. Sometimes there are delays in activation. "Give it time," the storeowner told him.

"Answer me!"

Bhe continued to send out a barrage of messages to Regie. He received these, but couldn't respond. There was a tug-of-war between Bhe and the boss, between family and things. It wasn't simple. In Regie's mind and in the reality he lived in, he was entrusted—at the car lot—with items of great value. To violate that trust would jeopardize future jobs. Yet he was here working to meet his family's needs and they needed him at home. His struggle was simplified to family need against family need.

Bhe's silent phone oppressed her. She sent message after message. She threatened separation. She meant separation. The phone that didn't ring back was a stone in her hand. She wanted to squeeze an answer out of it, or at least hear Regie's voice. She could do neither. She felt broken, by the storm, by her poverty—one hundred pesos (two dollars) would get her home—and by Regie's disregard. She curled up in a ball in the empty classroom and held her knees.

Chris and I delivered food to a Pastor at a barangay just a few kilometers from here. The pastor, the wife and three hundred kids were jumping around on the slab of the church—all that remains. The community is a muddy torn up mess, a shantytown, and a remnant of Typhoon Yolanda that has left people more vulnerable than ever before.

—From an aid worker's journal, 2014, Tacloban, Philippines

C H A P T E R   1

An Uncertain Calm

D A N A   L A B I T A

At 7:00 am Danovie (Dana) Labita, a registered nurse, finishes her night duty. She works in Tacloban caring for an elderly Chinese woman who is bedridden and virtually comatose. Her patient is kept alive with various medical apparatuses, including a nasogastric feeding tube. The patient is the matriarch of a successful business family who have holdings in a range of companies, including telecommunications, utilities, Tacloban Doctors Hospital, and in the past, one of the largest grocery retailers in Tacloban, Lee's Grocery. Dana's ninety-two-year-old patient lives with her two elderly sisters, who are seventy-seven and eighty-two, respectively. The most capable of the three is Dr. Adela Lay, the eighty-two year old, recently returned to Tacloban from New York City, to live with and care for her sisters. All three need some element of care. They employ four fulltime nurses, two per twelve hour shift, seven days a week.

Dana is their favorite. She is a professional nurse with seven years of international experience and she is fun. She brings to their home a unique blend of spirit and compassion. She has smiling eyes, an easy laugh and she is comfortable with Dr. Lay, having lived in an American compound in Saudi Arabia. The sisters feel lucky to have her.

"Dana, are you leaving?" asked Dr. Lay.

"Getting ready to, the storm is coming."

"Yes it is. Here is fifteen hundred pesos for the kids."

"Thank you."

"Get them something nice from the market. Take their minds off the typhoon."

Before Dana left she visited her comatose patient, who she called Mommu. "Mommu," Dana whispered. "Dana is leaving now. You will be okay. Father has prayed for you."

Every Wednesday Father Monsignor Abarce visited the Lay sisters and prayed for Mommu. Father Monsignor is from the Diocese of the Archbishop of Palo. This attention from the Diocese of Palo is something a poor person would never receive, but the Lay family are benefactors of the church.

"Bye Dr Lay," Dana called. "Tell Mom Edin bye." Mom Edin was the other sister. Dana gave Mommu one last brush across her forehead. Touch was part of Dana's understanding of healing.

"Yes I will. Buy something nice now," answered Dr. Lay.

"Yes, I will."

The Lay family did their best to include Dana in their family. Fifteen hundred pesos was a special gift, but they also gave in other ways. They insisted Dana eat with them, at the same table and the same food. This was not a usual situation for nurses in wealthy Filipino homes, but the Lays believed that the best service came out of respect and relationship.

Dana could not wait to get home to be a mother. Every moment home for Dana was a time of restoration. She had worked seven years in Saudi Arabia as an emergency room nurse. Eight hours a day she had dealt with death and the horribly injured. The Arab people in the Saudi hospitals were harsh and demanding, but this had been insignificant compared to the isolation and loneliness she had felt being separated from her family. The children did not know their mother, not the way she wanted them to know her.

To work overseas is the Filipino "lucky curse," her lucky curse. Dana felt she had been ambushed by her country, impoverished to the point she had to sell her motherhood for sustenance. And she didn't feel she was alone as a Filipino. Two years ago she had made a choice. She chose poverty and motherhood. She came home to Tacloban. Working for the Lays was, at the least, dignified poverty and she was near her children.

Dana took the short walk to Real Boulevard and paid eight pesos for a jeepney ride to her home in Paraiso, Barangay 83, San Jose. The jeepney was full. She sat between two other women. One was large, loud and smelled of fish. This woman kept talking of the typhoon. She was worried. Dana was glad to get off. She stopped at a small market just outside their street and bought some stickers for her children's notebooks. The streets were still quiet. Only a few people were about. There was a light rain falling, which was refreshing in the heat, but dirty on the ground. Tacloban sat between two bays, the Panalaran Bay and the Cancabato Bay. Her barangay or barrio was at the foot of Cancabato Bay. It was a narrow slip of land, heavily populated. Dana was glad to be home early before the crush of roadside humanity. She slipped into their home. The children were still sleeping; her husband Allan was preparing breakfast.

Dana showered, the cold water refreshing her skin, sweaty from the humidity and heat. She washed off the jeepney dirt and the clammy closeness of unidentified humanity. She took her time, glad to feel the cool water splash like a baptism over and over, washing away her worries, cleaning her for this precious gift of motherhood.

Eight-year-old Ax was there. "Mama what did you bring me?" he asked.

"Well....I brought you a movie." She decided to save the stickers for later.

"What is it?"

Dana pulled out a movie called the Pulchet Tragedy. This was a favorite of the family and especially of Ax. The hero was a boy called Dante, who was engulfed by a tsunami many times but survived. Dante always amazed Ax. He was Ax's hero.

"I don't want to watch it."

"Why not?" She reached over to hold him close. He pulled away. He did not like touch, at least hers. Ax walked outside and looked around.

Dana watched Ax through the open door. He was afraid of everything she thought. He was afraid of the leaves going back and forth. Afraid of the dog. Afraid of what he imagined. Afraid of her leaving again. Ax would often sit and think. He would lie at night looking at the ceiling, not sleeping.

The Pulchet Tragedy was really a movie for Dana. Seeing Ax she was immediately full of premonitions and fears. Her early morning ride home packed among strangers on the jeepney, each keeping to themselves and their thoughts, except for the large woman, the gifts at the market, the tired walk down her side street, her mother-in-law up now and sitting on her chair reciting the Rosary, the thoughts of preparation for the coming typhoon and the years of loneliness and separation weighed her down. She wanted this story for herself. Watching little Ax, hair tousled, eyes still full of sleepers, stand outside gazing at the sky, she wanted reassurance. She wanted to believe in their safety. She wanted to recapture her lost years in every moment.

Just over a year before on August 10, 2012 8:00 pm, Tacloban was hit with a 7.2 earthquake. Dana remembered it just so. Dinner was over. The children were watching X-men on the TV. She was washing dishes. Allan was in the bathroom. He came out of the comfort room just as the earthquake hit. As a family they evacuated, per her direction, to the bedroom and she began to pray, quietly at first, then louder and louder until she was shouting at God to make the ground stop shaking. Ax was trembling and hugging her. Allan wanted to go outside, but Dana insisted they stay. "No!" she yelled. "No!" Looking back she thought of her faith that had taken them to a place of danger. She had known then that God would keep them safe, that the angel God would be there to protect them, but now she did not trust herself. She had strong faith, but maybe it was dangerous to have strong faith. She tended to misuse it and test God.

During the earthquake neighbors around them had been shouting and crying. Afterwards Allan had said wryly "That maybe next time the praying should happen outside, where the roof will not land on our heads."

Dana remembered the earthquake, Allan her husband, Ax and his fear and her fear as well, but mostly of her faith in safety, in her God, the protector of them. Dana watched Ax, her child with a weak personality.

The morning was a day of sun and light rain. The wind seemed to Dana slow and solemn, turning like a big wheel. "It's coming Allan, it's coming Allan," she said.

But in another moment she tried to convince herself that it wasn't. "If this is so strong, why is it silent and the sun is out?" Back and forth she argued with herself, silently and with Allan. The days before Yolanda had been days of worry. This time of Yolanda preparation was the culmination of it. There had been a lot of discussion and a lot of apprehension. All week the sun had shown. At night the sliver of a moon had hung silent and visible. Dana remembered again the earthquake; the fear, the wild prayers, and she clung onto her religion of a God that would not permit destruction of their home or their lives, just as in the earthquake, no damage and no hurt.

Allan and she were at odds. He kept saying, "You have to focus yourself. You have to understand the meaning of the weather forecast. You will do this for your safety."

She and Allan had different perceptions on their faith. Allan would say, "I do not rely on Him. He has His part and I have mine. I have to take my part. I cannot expect Him to do it. He has given me eyes, nose, ears..."

"Yes, and those are gifts," Dana would interject.

"It is what I am have been given, but also what I have to use," he would reply.

So in spite of her faith—a faith she knew from childhood that required obedience to ritual and offered safety in return—that wrestled with her husband's faith of human responsibility and didn't lose, it only rested, she began to prepare for the coming storm. She lit a candle to Santo Niño and she put together an emergency kit, a bag of clothes, food, water, milk, diapers, jackets, rubber shoes, raincoats, and medical supplies.

Allan watched the TV and monitored the storm's progress.

Last night the wind blew; a tropical storm was forecast to hit us. It sounded like our barn roof when I was a boy sleeping in the hayloft on a summer night, crashes of tin as loose pieces of sheeting were pried by the wind and then slammed back down. In the distance it sounded like gunshots as roofing hanging on with tired nails struggled to survive, a tug-of-war, back and forth between the wind and the roof. This was Tacloban, dark, windy, wet, the ravages of the storm banging its way through the night.

—From an aid worker's journal, 2014, Tacloban, Philippines

C H A P T E R   2

The Waiting

S A M U E L   M A G D U A

Between 5:00 and 11:00 pm, Samuel the fisherman, watched the TV monitoring the movements of the typhoon. Around them half the families evacuated, but past him in the heavily populated area of his barangay most of the people stayed. Samuel knew the population of Barangay 88. He has lived here all his life. It is well over double the official census of ten thousand. Twenty-two thousand people are jammed into this community. He is not sure why the government pretends otherwise. It is not just his community. All the census numbers are under reported. Only the registered are counted and what are squatters? They are unregistered, unmarried and unborn, yet they live too.

Samuel's faith was far from personal. He prayed to God every day, but only in generalities and lived his life in such a way to keep God comfortably distant. But this night—as he watched the news and the reports of winds exceeding three hundred kilometers an hour—he changed. He prayed that this typhoon would skip the earth and launch itself into heaven. He prayed continually into the night. He prayed specifics—"God, save us all, change the direction of this storm, save us God"—something new for him.

Yet when Geraldine began packing and preparing clothes and talking about evacuation, Samuel resisted. He did not want to go and did not want his wife to go.

"What are you doing?" he asked. "We aren't going."

Geraldine stopped and looked at him. "What about the typhoon?" she said.

"We are fine here. Look at the weather. There is no wind."

"But the TV?"

For a man like Samuel who spent his life on the open sea, in a boat he had built with his own hands and lived in a home he had constructed over a period of years, the idea of being herded like sheep to a school or a hall was ultimate submission. For him it was not safety, it was captivity. He feared the wind and the coming typhoon, but he feared more the wind in the confines of other men. And he truly believed in his boat on the water, his home on the land. So in his heart he prayed and with his body he bullied his wife into staying.

"To hell with the TV. I will stay here regardless. Go if you want, but I am staying. Sheila Mae will stay too."

At 10:00 pm, the last of the official evacuation had finished. Fifty percent of his neighbors had chosen to ride out the storm in their homes. The other fifty percent had walked to local evacuation centers, schools and barangay halls. A few had gone to the astrodome. Some of the wealthy had left Tacloban. The people in charge of the evacuation were gone. They had come in various vehicles. All told, approximately six vehicles had arrived to evacuate 22,000 people in an afternoon and evening. The evacuation vehicles had left half full.

Rene and Imbit returned from the sea. They had experienced strong winds and growing swells and had made the wise choice to return to shore. It was not that the winds were too strong, or the swells too big, it was the dearth of life, the birds that flew in flocks past them to the west. It was the quietness that was too quiet to be peaceful. It was a savage serenity. They had cast their nets and were trawling like a normal day, but at some point as if they were in one boat and one mind, they both hurriedly pulled in their nets and "tough guys" that they were, their toughness disappeared in the face of the coming typhoon. Their engines choked and cried and carried them to shore. There was no one to meet them when they returned. But there were people about talking in small clusters.

"Is it coming?" Someone asked Imbit as he secured his boat.

"Yes," he said.

Samuel watched the news. He did not see Rene and Imbit return, but he thought of them quietly, regretting his words, "They are just committing suicide." His heart felt like a clam in his chest, and the mussel inside moved slowly and seemed at times to stop altogether. It was too late to leave and he had no place he wanted to go.

He lay down to sleep. Geraldine lay beside him, as did Sheila May. They slept in one room. Samuel dozed off first though it took a while. Geraldine found comfort in his solid back, wrapping one arm around his chest.

"I love you," she whispered.

We have been covering the salaries of four people at the foundation, Honey, Ruth and two young men. Yesterday afternoon, three strangers with ski masks, shot the father of one of the young men in the head, eight times. The family is not sure why he was killed or who killed him. His dad was shot in the province where he lived.

I know how I feel about this. I feel murderous too. In this time of great social tragedy the political and personal conflicts, which are so petty and so temporary, rise up with particular ugliness. There is no excuse to kick a dog on a rope, to act on vanities when all that was vain was destroyed, but immorality seems to have blossomed among those with a leaning toward evil and diminish in those with a propensity for good.

—From an aid worker's journal, 2014, Tacloban, Philippines

CHAPTER 2

The Waiting

NOEL LITO

At 2:00 pm, the Baptist Pastor arrived and a few of the prisoners gathered for a one-hour bible study. This was something Noel, while in jail, had been attending for a few years. Noel liked the Baptists. He liked Pastor Matthew who came. He liked the jokes and freedom that were present. He was not yet baptized—maybe that would come later—but he was a believer.

At 3:00 pm, the Seventh Day Adventists came for an hour. Noel attended this service as well. He listened intently, reverently, finding peace in the safety of the room and in his conversion. He had a bible and he followed the teaching. This was his routine and his safety. He was not a proselytizer; he would have needed more confidence or a need to convince himself. He had no confidence and he was convinced. A prison is a lonely place and his relationship with God—deeply private, impossible to share—was a shelter. How could he turn his inside out for others to see? He couldn't see it himself, he couldn't articulate it and he needed it where it was, in a room of armor.

At 5:00 pm, in the city jail there is a mandatory Catholic rosary for all the prisoners, which is conducted by one of the inmates. The priests do not come, only the beads are pulled out and for the next hour the rise and fall of the incantations of the incarcerated fill the air. They started with three Hail Mary prayers, moved into the Glory Be to the Father prayer and the Apostles Creed. Some of the prisoners fingered their cross. The Lord's Prayer was recited five times, one for each of the five large beads and then the mysteries were meditated upon. This being Thursday, the Luminous Mystery signifying the transfiguration of Christ floated ghost like in the courtyard. Hail Mary prayers were said on each of the ten small beads and more Glory Be to the Father prayers filled the air and the incarcerated closed with the litany of the Blessed Virgin Mary. Twelve hundred voices rising and falling, shouting, singing, together, apart, a powerful emotional choir of convicted and un-convicted men and women who in this moment shared a common captivity with their countrymen and their God, bound together by the Holy Rosary.

When it was over dusk had arrived. The sun had slipped away like a tired altar boy to his bed. Noel filed back to his room for lock-up. The coming typhoon, the preparations of his relatives outside the walls, the TV broadcasters and the laughter of the evening lights did not exist to him. His cell was black. There was a light breeze blowing.

Noel lay in his bunk dreaming about life, specifically Maricris—his thoughts were always coming back to Maricris—but other things too, childhood memories that he used to occupy his mind. The afternoon and early evening of faith teachings were always there, floating phantom-like. He thought about the teaching from Pastor Matt, "Jesus Redeemed the World." The world—a place peopled—seemed so far away, so untouchable, too big to understand, too corrupted to be redeemed.

He had no concern about the coming typhoon. He felt well protected. The guards had made no special arrangements. There was no TV or news of any sort available to the prisoners. It was a quiet evening. There were no arguments. This was just another night in the city jail. It was close to his two-thousandth night.

At 9:00 pm, there was some scuffling and a few moans from a

corner of the room. It was a common nightly interruption. He lay frozen, listening, hoping the urge of another man wouldn't rise up and use him.

He thought about his coming child, concentrating on the swollen belly of Maricris and shut out thoughts of her father who did not know they were "married." He thought about his childhood, but specific thoughts, like the rolling tire he played with, keeping it going round and round and round with a stick. Slowly and carefully he fought the night sounds and concentrated gently on the good things, until sleep, blessed sleep, overtook him and the moaning disappeared.

On Sunday the Church had some evangelists from Laguna Bay, near Cainta arrived. They were a team of Filipinos with one American fellow. The American fellow was a throwback to the traveling evangelist. He spoke loud, repetitiously and stuttered his sentences and words. I disliked it of course and so did not respond to the calls. They asked for hand raising. I did not raise my hand. They asked for people to stand up. I did not stand up. In fact I was the only person who did not stand up in the whole dang church. I looked around and everybody was standing. Everybody was cheering.

After the service young pastor Jake, who had been sitting behind me, looked me in the eye with a quizzical look. It was not a judgmental look but I felt judged anyway. I tried to process my reaction on the way home. I did not say anything to anybody, but I felt eyes in my back. Eyes sometimes reside in my back, peering through the flesh into and through me, like I was a shadow of who I should be. Eyes are guilt, when they are on my back looking from behind.

But now I feel better. These men, bearing gifts and coercion are taking two boys, Alfredo 12 and Sonny 15 to Laguna to study at their school.

So I sent Dess our social worker, and Jake with the inquisitive eyes to talk to the boys and the boy's parents, and later I went too. The father was concerned, but he was not sure if he was allowed to say no. We assured him he was and he was relived. The dynamics of the scam, if that is what it is, plays on all the complex emotions and fears that I myself felt in church. Things sound so good, nothing is wrong, yet something isn't right. Everyone else is exalting. Why not I? I should stand because standing before God is good is it not, and so should my son go to school should he not.

But with the boys, the trap goes deeper. There is the social dynamic of dealing with a powerful white man. There are the multiple gifts the men have brought to the home.

We talked to one of the boys. He has a chin that fades away and a soft pliable look to him. I have heard that those who prey can spot the easy prey and Sonny looked like easy prey to me. He wanted to go to Laguna, no doubts, and his sister had given him permission. She was twenty-five and had a family. Sonny lives with her, so we called the sister.

"How did you feel when they brought the gifts to your house?" Dess asked.

"I felt like they were payment for my brother," she said. "They wanted to take our sister too."

"Your sister, how old is your sister?"

"She is eleven."

Today Dess will report these men to the Department of Social Welfare and Development.

I must struggle with my own demons, a zeal to believe in the guilt of these men, as a form of redemption, for the guilt I felt during their Sunday show.

Dess went to the Department of Social Welfare and Development to verify if our trafficking concerns were legitimate, knowing they were, and they were. The DSWD took Dess to the Women and Child Protection Services at the police station, where the DSWD filed a report.

"Where are they from?" The police asked.

"Laguna."

"Laguna!' He smashed his fist on the table. *"We have too many reports on Laguna."*

I must stand on the fact that these men— whatever their ultimate intentions good or bad— were attempting something illegal, and they were attempting it in a way that was manipulative and obligatory. They did everything wrong and they did it as a trafficker would do it. Promises, gifts, and from a position of power.

—From an aid worker's journal, 2014, Tacloban, Philippines

C H A P T E R   2

The Waiting

A L L A N   L A B I T A

Allan's afternoon, as his morning, was devoted to typhoon preparations. He did not feel anxious, just different. At two o'clock he watched as the clouds far above began to pick up speed and he observed flocks of birds migrating south, birds he did not recognize and migrations that did not normally happen. He understood more than his neighbors about a storm surge. He had tried to explain that typically it would be a rising of the ocean as the wind pushed it along, but he did not understand it completely. The reports were discussing an eight to fifteen foot surge, which to him and those he talked about it with, was just a big wave and big waves were a regular sight on the ocean. Their home in San Jose was over one kilometer from the shore, what damage could a fifteen-foot wave do? He could not imagine any.

Uncle Alex and Allan discussed preparations for later that evening and decided that everyone should evacuate to Uncle Alex's residence, which was concrete and adjacent to Allan's. They talked over their common fence, the one with orchids. They leaned on it, one on one side. One on the other.

"The winds are projected to be over two hundred kilometers," said Allan.

"Everyone should come here Friday morning before it hits," said Uncle Alex. "I will have food and water here, but you should have everyone bring some blankets and pillows."

"What about flooding? I am putting everything up in the rafters."

"If it floods, we could go to the next door neighbors." But I think our biggest concern is the wind, flying debris, and the food and water afterwards. We will be safe here, or if worse comes to worst we can always go next door."

Later on Thursday the TV newscasters revised the time of the storm's arrival to eleven o'clock Friday morning. Allan and Uncle decided the children and some of the women should plan to spend the night at Uncle's house. Uncle Alex spent the afternoon setting up accommodations for an additional fourteen people. His home was not big; besides the kitchen and comfort room, he had a small bedroom and a large sala, which he re-arranged to accommodate the additional five children and three women. Allan's wife, Dana, would be working and Uncle Alex knew his sister, Allan's mom, would not leave her own bed.

Allan's mother always had coffee at 3:00 pm. It was her bonding time with whomever was there. For Allan it was often bittersweet. Thursday Allan's mother was re-arranging the statues of the Saints, something she rarely did. Allan could tell she was worried, so he left her alone.

Allan and his mother's latest conflict was fresh in both their minds. The San Jose Festival was coming on May 25, still months away, but the Women's Catholic League, CWL, had visited everyone in the barangay and delivered a letter requesting payment from each family to cover the fiesta expenses. This requested amount was based on CWL's perception of the family's income. Allan's family, considered middle class, was supposed to give one thousand pesos.

Allan and his mother had argued about the fiesta offering.

"Read this," his mother had said. "It is a letter from the church."

"What is this? They are asking you to give a defined amount?"

"It is about the church. Let's give it."

"I don't like it; it is the obligation. It is not right for them to tell us how much to give."

"It is okay with me, it is for the good of the church, for Jesus."

"I don't believe it. It is not for Jesus. It is just a renovation, a thirty-year renovation that has never been done. Mom, don't pay it. It is not right."

Allan and his mother have had a tendency to argue about many things, but especially the church. Where his mother prayed openly and often on her rosaries, Allan prayed quietly and simply. In the past he had asked many things from God, but nothing happened, so he began to pray differently. He did not ask for things, except perhaps strength, and he thanked God for the day, very briefly. He had read some books about Jesus and it seemed to him that what Jesus did was different from the churches, so he changed. He still went to church with his mom, but only as a tradition, not as a faith. Others in the family were not so vocal as Allan. If they thought about faith or God they kept their thoughts to themselves. They did not cross their mother.

Dana, Allan's wife, did not get involved in Allan's discussions with his mother, but Dana and Allan struggled to find common ground in their beliefs. Dana, who was brought up in Catholic schools, had been trained to trust that God would work everything out; she only a passive believer in Him. Allan, on the other hand, would say, "We must act. God doesn't always punish the wicked or reward the righteous. If we do not confront bad people, they will grow stronger and our family will be at risk. We must be involved. We must do something about it."

At 4:00 pm, Allan and Dana went to the fish market, a five-minute pedicab ride from their house. He talked to a few people at the market and the word "storm surge" kept coming up. Everyone was confused by its meaning. Dana picked up a few spices. The stalls were crowded and people were panic buying.

At 6:00 pm, Thursday evening, twelve of the family, Allan, Dana, Armida, Arnel, Kim, Arman, Mother, baby Coleen, Phill, Yugi, Ax and Bridgette were home, all except Aileen and Tina, who were both still working. The evening news was on. Everyone took turns watching the reports. The winds were projected to reach two hundred and eighty-five kilometers an hour. There was little conversation. They ate an early supper so it would give them more time to relocate to their uncle's. The sun had set and other than a few lights and the moon it was pitch black outside.

At 6:15 pm, Aileen arrived with a box of pizza; she was exhausted from her day at the office. Dana bustled around getting ready to leave for her twelve-hour shift. She kissed all the kids. All but Ax. She didn't even bother to ask him. Everyone hated to see Dana leave. Mother asked if it was necessary.

Allan walked outside with her and they stood together for a moment. "*Makadi na ako*," she said, which means, "I will go now."

Allan watched her leave. She disappeared into the night, down the road to the main street and the jeepney stop. She was swinging her hips as she does, the moon helping to light her path. He stood there for ten minutes looking at the sky, listening to the wind.

Allan didn't know why, but he called Dana five minutes later. Perhaps he longed for her voice, or maybe the affection of their youth. The idea that she was leaving and she would be gone, another time when mother was absent; perhaps when she was needed most, his were just a jumble of thoughts, of nostalgia and concern.

"Do you really have to leave tonight? ...Your relief might not show up tomorrow because of the typhoon...."

"I am on the jeepney now. Do you want me to come back?"

"Would it be okay?"

"It's fine... so do I have to stop the jeepney to get back there?"

The question hung in the air, she waited and he waited—she hoped he would tell her to come—he stammered out a reply. "Go on, be safe and I will see you tomorrow."

"Okay," she said.

Allan stepped back into the bustle of the home. Everyone was making preparations to move to Uncle Alex's house. Ax was afraid. Allan kissed his forehead and told him to "Get up and be tough, we'll be fine, I am here with you."

Tina arrived about 8:00 pm, so everyone was there except Dana, thirteen in all. It was agreed that the four brothers, Allan, Kim, Arnel, Arman and mother would sleep at the Labita family house, leaving the five children and three sisters with Allan's uncle, aunt and Sing-Sing, his aunt's seventeen-year-old niece.

It was a busy time. Dana texted to check on the kids and make sure the transfer had happened. Allan texted back that everything was done. They bid each other goodnight.

He walked outside and stood around with some of the fellows from the community. They discussed the typhoon, but nobody seemed worried.

"I'll just swim along with the tide when the so-called storm surge comes," one laughed.

Allan walked back inside. Arnel and Kim were sleeping on the sofa. He lay on an easy chair and peered up through the window to the sky. There was no sign of bad weather. He thought it odd, the calmness. It felt so different. He turned the radio down. The broadcaster was still calling for evacuation, but that opportunity was long past. He prayed to Jesus to protect them from anything and everything odd that might happen… then he thanked Him… as he always did.

Walter Brueggemann in his book *Prophetic Imagination*, correlates Economics of Affluence – Politics of Oppression – Religion of Immanence (that of a captive God).

I think of Dana, who lost her son Ax and her words were, "this is not part of my religion. God cannot do this to my family." Her religion has been one of a captive God, and, as Brueggeman says, it is necessary to maintain (Philippine) society that this is so. How could Filipinos live with the "economics of affluence" and "politics of oppression" with a God who does not support the affluent and the oppressors?

Gone from the Philippines is a Jesus who hates oppression, shouts out for justice, and who shuns affluence. Dana's captive God was washed away in Yolanda, but will He stay banished, or be reborn, again subservient to her religion? If He doesn't come back the servant—to affluence, oppression and captivity—but free, Philippine society itself can be changed.

—From an aid worker's journal, 2014, Tacloban, Philippines

C H A P T E R   2

The Waiting

D O L O R   L I N G O

A t 6:00 pm Thursday, the Lingo's ate their last meal together as a family. The meal was simple: noodles and rice. There was no fish because most of the fisherman had not been out for a week. Dolor's neighbors will fish occasionally, but the weather reports are so unreliable that the majority of the men in her community do not venture out the week of a storm. Too many have been lost.

The four children—Daniel, Dante Jr., David Carl and Princess Diana—were excited, because they were shortly being transferred to Grandmother's big house on the ocean. They often slept there, but it was still a holiday treat. Grandmother, whose name was Constellation, had been preparing for the grandchildren, and even for her children, if they chose to come, which some of them would.

The walk to Grandmother's house was not even a walk. It was just around the corner, past three bundled together homes. It took just a minute and the six of them walked together.

"To Grandmother's house we go," sang David Carl.

Dante carried Princess Diana, but only because he wanted to. Dante Jr. skipped ahead.

"Hi mom," Dolor said when they got there.

Constellation didn't respond directly. She was hugging the children. She had seen them during the day, just as she saw them every day, but this was a special event, camping out at Grandma's.

"Let's see, I think the four of you will sleep in the back kitchen," she said to Daniel the oldest. "Follow me."

There were a total of sixteen, without Dolor and Dante, spending the night at Grandmother's: Grandmother, Dolor's brother's family of six, her sister's family—the barangay official—of five and the four Lingo children. There was some light-hearted discussion about the typhoon. No one was concerned. The massive foundation of Grandmother's house had withstood years of beating and with the latest addition was stronger than ever. The storm surge was discussed but not understood. The word surge was not in Dolor's language, there was no translation, only the English word bantered about by the radio and TV broadcasters and mixed in with the local Waray dialect. It was a word the announcers did not know themselves, but was repeated as it was given, by rote.

"I haven't even listened to the news," Dolor volunteered. "What's the latest?"

"It's a typhoon," her sister Nanita said. "I have been busy telling people to leave and yet here we are."

"The news says there is a storm surge."

"Must mean strong storm," someone said.

"Oh well, Dante and I will be safe in our beds. The kids will have fun here."

Dante and Dolor walked back to their hidden home. The night was mild, the winds light. A few neighbors were out, some were walking to the barangay hall. Dolor called to them and waved. "Our children are safe at Constellation's," she called.

At 9:00 pm Thursday evening Dolor and Dante crawled into bed. The humidity was ninety plus and the temperature hovered around 30 degrees Celsius. It was a normal evening in Leyte.

"Shall we pray?" she asked Dante.

"Yes, go ahead."

She prayed for the children, for her extended family, for Dante and herself and for safety from the coming storm. Eventually she prayed Dante asleep. His quiet breathing was the only sound in their protected home. Her last thought was of the children, safe at her mother's.

Erickson makes ice at night. This morning he sleeps on two chairs, mummified in a blanket. Erickson was at the Foundation Building by the bay when the storm surge hit. The Foundation Building was reinforced concrete, one story, with multiple rooms. Today it is not even rubble as that has been removed. It is just a couple of stray pillars and some bamboo where we had constructed a short-lived tent. Erickson survived. He is small and thin, with no fat. Sinews of muscle cover his bones. He was washed to and fro like sand in a sieve until the building was gone and he was able to grab the overhead power lines. He clung to those, while the water whirled him left and right. At the end he had a power line badge around his waist, raw and red.

—From an aid worker's journal, 2014, Tacloban, Philippines

CHAPTER 2

The Waiting

CARLITO QUIAS

The ocean was close enough to Clarito's house to hit a baseball to. It licked the shore. The sun shone intermittently. The family of fifteen relaxed and talked, discussing the storm, the radio sounding its alarm in the background. A few neighbors were preparing to evacuate later that night. The Quias family talked about evacuating, but the family was divided. Claring, Clarito's wife, was a domineering woman, strong minded and purposeful. She epitomized the matriarchal society of the Filipinos, where women make decisions and men with passive aggression acquiesce.

Women are safer—in public, as poor people—than men. They can safely stand up to authority and resist. They can cross their arms and stand immobile when their squatter rights are violated. They will not suffer, or be subject to the same abuse and careless unconcern that men experience. In the face of the police, who are mostly male, men are far more vulnerable to physical and emotional mistreatment than women. Perhaps this alone, this ability to stand up for their men and families, this power of matriarchal gender in poor Filipino society, slips subtly into the family as well, where authority has come to be dominated by one sex.

71

Carlito accepts his subservient role in his household and society. He thinks little of it, though it pervades his whole being. His world is one of escape paths, little ways to forget what he has been made to do, but cannot. He likes his unfiltered cigarettes and the biting smoke in his lungs. He likes his pedicabs and the small income he earns. He likes his Tanduay rum. He even likes his quiet rebellious thoughts as if thoughts alone could give him back his manhood. He lives the dual life of a poor Filipino man in differing levels of surrender. For Carlito his surrender is mostly complete. He has surrendered to his wife and his resistance stops there. She is his obstacle and his protector. The government and the powerful are too far removed to be part of his rebellion.

As the day progressed and the radio continued to fill their home with warnings and forebodings the family separated into two decisive camps. Carlito wanted to evacuate as did Elna, Jun's wife.

Rex, Carlito's son, told his father quietly, "I will only go if you go Dad. I will not leave you."

"You should go," Carlito whispered back. "I have to stay with Claring."

Claring, undeterred by the commentaries and the warnings of the radio, was adamant they stay. Claring's children followed their mother's lead, except for Jun, Elna's husband. He was torn between two women and so in silence kept his counsel to himself.

"What are you afraid of?" Claring asked Carlito. "If our roof flies off our things are still here."

Carlito kept silent, his voiceless rebellion only a shadow on his face. There was no sense in talking, no sense in arguing. He just listened to the news, his heart heavy, his fear growing. Claring was scornful. The children for the most part docile.

The afternoon was odd. The zeal of the radio announcers clashed with the relative calm of the day.

"We are not going anywhere," Claring said again and again.

Carlito did not answer her. There was no use. He listened to her and listened to the radio. He took walks out to the ocean, sipping his cigarette, letting the smoke fill his throat and lungs, holding it there, like he held his fear and then releasing the smoke, letting it flow gently out his lungs, through his throat, wafting between his teeth and open lips. It was spiritual to him, the inhaling and the letting go. He found a semblance of peace. "Thank God for cigarettes," he said to himself.

"Look at the weather. What do they know?" Claring said.

She could not let it go. She knew Carlito disagreed and she also knew without doubt she was in the right. Her family, children, grandchildren and husband would be safe here in their home by the ocean, as they had been for the last fifty years and her mother before them. Wind, water, tropical storms and typhoons came season after season. It was a way of life. It was what she knew.

The family ate a dinner, quiet except for the radio in the background.

"We should turn that damn thing off," Claring said once, but no one did.

At 11:00 pm on Thursday, Jun, Elna and the two boys, Cyron and Sandro, left for the Astrodome. Elna had won out. Claring did not say a word. She was lying down, but she was not sleeping. The evacuation had become personal for her.

Clarito followed Jun and Elna out when they evacuated. They carried a change of clothes, two water bottles, crackers and some blankets. The sun had been down for five hours. There were no stars. The few streetlights cast dim yellow marbles of light on the road. They loaded their belongings on one of Carlito's pedicabs. He watched them go, the pedicab rising and falling over the ruts of the road, like a drunk full of *tuba*.

He checked on his personal pedicab. He checked it because he didn't want any one taking it for evacuation, even his wife's children. He checked to make sure it was locked tightly. He rattled the chain and glanced around. The few things he owned he treasured and he didn't share.

At midnight Carlito checked on his pedicab again and again at 1:00 am. There were a number of neighbors milling about. They were gathering last minute belongings, leaving the coast, frightened by the news the TV announcers were reporting. Children—too tired to cry—were standing in small sleepy bundles, waiting for parents. The waves on the sea were rolling in and collapsing on the sand in a steady rhythm. The wind felt stronger. It smelled of salt and felt thickly humid. Carlito breathed it in, sucking it heavily—the anxiety of the neighborhood, and the fear of a typhoon coming, somewhere out there, stirring the ocean, was like the breathing of a Samar cigar— dark, ripe, and sickening. Carlito did not talk to anyone. They were all busy with their belongings and their children and he was busy pretending to fiddle with his pedicab.

"You are not going to sleep," his wife said when he came in.

"I will just stay here and watch the news," Carlito replied.

"Okay just stay there," she said, the anger hanging cold in the air.

Just after 1:00 am the neighbors—who were leaving—had left. Rain was falling, light and intermittent. The wind was rustling the coconut palms. Carlito went to sleep. His last thought was that they should leave, all leave, but there was no use convincing his wife.

All of Eastern Samar that we have seen
has been destroyed by the typhoon. Where I sit is
once where over thirty houses dotted the beach. I
see sign of only one. My computer sits on a broken
slab of it. The beach lost over four feet of sand
and one hundred feet of coconut trees. Where
the wind and ocean did not tear up trees, then it
twisted and broke them off. It is much like walking
through a mountaintop woods recently clear-cut,
stubs—stumps and lying logs are all that are left.
The forest soil is coated with the seedy ocean sand.
The gutted beachfront is scattered like grain on the
ground of this timbered land.
  —Visiting the Pacific coast of Eastern
Samar, from an aid worker's journal, 2014,
Tacloban, Philippines

C H A P T E R   2

The Waiting

R E G I E   P A A

At the car lot Regie watched the TV. He listened to the reports coming in from the different stations. The storm was bigger than he had imagined. "It is heading for us and then for my family," he told Wendell.

"I am leaving." Regie finally told Wendell. "I don't care anymore." But he didn't leave.

He tried. He walked to the nearby Van service, named Van Vans. They were open, but had suspended all services. And that was the story at every traveling company in Tacloban. He walked from Van Vans to Duptours to Grandtours, kilometer after kilometer, and as he walked the afternoon slipped away. The sun sank into the grey clouds, the birds flew west and south, and the wind blew gently. Bhe said her goodbyes. It was 5:00 pm when Regie returned to the car lot. He put his phone—he couldn't use—on silent, and did not read any more messages from his wife. The one hundred and ten kilometers to home seemed like the other side of the world.

The land Regie's car lot was on was owned by Kuya Boy, who lived just behind the lot in a cement house. Between Kuya Boy's house and the car lot were two smaller homes, one vacant and one occupied by Bobby, Kuya Boy's yard help. The smaller homes were ramshackle dwellings of cheap lumber, but the main house sat on a solid three-foot raised foundation. It looked like a Craftsman home, with thick walls, porches and heavy windows. Kuya Boy and Bobby came over to the Car lot around 6:00 pm, something they occasionally did.

"Hey guys," Kuya Boy said.

"Hello Kuya Boy." Wendell and Regie answered.

"Regie, here is some money, run and get some San Miguel." Kuya Boy handed Regie four crumpled one-hundred peso bills.

Beer sounded pretty good to Regie. He was hot and sweaty from traversing Tacloban looking for a ride and he was frustrated and worried, all things beer could help with. He hustled over to the *sari-sari* store and purchased a case, six one-liter bottles, of San Miguel.

Wendell, Regie, Bobby and Kuya Boy sat around and drank beer and discussed the coming typhoon. All except Bobby, who didn't have anything to say, he just poured the beer, happy to drink it.

"They are saying a fifteen meter storm surge," said Kuya Boy.

"What does that mean?" asked Wendell.

"It doesn't matter," said Kuya Boy. "Tacloban is a sheltered area. "Between the bay, the peninsula, and the mountains of Samar, Tacloban is naturally protected. And we are good here too."

The car lot and Kuya Boy's house are only a few hundred meters from the foot of Cancabato Bay. The round-a-bout it sits on connects the Pan-Philippine Highway, heading toward the San Juanico Bridge, the Tabuan National Highway that goes to Palo, the DZR (Daniel Z. Romualdez) Highway heading to the Airport, and the Maharlika Highway into Tacloban. The San Pedro Bay is 2.3 kilometers away. Regie knows this because he once drove a car there and checked the distance with the odometer. The San Pedro Bay disappears into the Leyte Gulf and the then to the Pacific Ocean. Together they make a deep wide mouthed funnel, narrowing to Tacloban.

Regie looked over toward the Coke Plant, it was barely visible through the Coconut Palms that shaded everything. "I wish I was home," he said.

Bobby poured some more beer, filling their glasses.

"You are welcome to evacuate to our house, later on, if you need to," said Kuya Boy.

"Okay," Regie said.

The beer and the conversation muted the TV, still spitting out its dire warnings in the background. The six-liters of San Miguel disappeared. The four men relaxed and laughed. The beer did its magic. Groups of men throughout the city drank to a storm they could not see, a warning they could not understand. They, like Regie and his friends, let the alcohol allay their worries and the storm and the coming typhoon—now a super typhoon, swirling around in the Pacific far away—did not seem real. Certainly no longer dangerous.

At 8:00 pm, Bobby and Kuya Boy left to go home. Regie watched a little more TV, but it was just sounds and pictures. It made no sense to him. At 9:00 pm he gave up and crawled into a Toyota Crosswind to sleep. He had his bag of clothes, some mineral water and his money, just in case the water rose. Wendell crawled into one of the other five cars, the one in the middle. Their day was over.

*My table is a slab of a house and my
seat is two broken blocks. I am sitting in a
community that is no more, a sea of homes that
was swallowed by an ocean and a devastating
wind. We left Tacloban yesterday. It was becoming
like Manila, with the never-ending bustle of life.
Our team needed respite so we drove to Eastern
Samar and the eastern shore. We drove for hours,
until the paved roads became partially paved and
pitted with ruts, and then we drove off the main
road to the ocean, to this community and this wide
expanse of beach with broken coconut palms and
survivors.*
      *—Visiting Samar, from an aid worker's
journal, 2014, Tacloban, Philippines*

C H A P T E R   2

The Waiting

D A N A   L A B I T A

Mixed in with Dana's day of struggle, preparation, worry and faith was a fair amount of joy and laughter. At three o'clock her best friend Rose stopped by with her husband Tully. They were car shopping and wanted Allan to go with them, because Allan knew a man at a dealership. Together the four of them visited the car lot and discussed the price. For Dana it felt like a normal time and that was a good thing.

Dana and Rose joked about the typhoon, though beneath Dana's joking was an acceptance that this was a strong storm. It was just too sunny and too ordinary for her to be somber.

The four embraced when they parted. "Good luck with Yolanda." Rose said.

"Tell Cliff to send me some chocolate." Dana yelled. Cliff is Rose's American brother-in-law.

"Yes, Yes." Rose responded and she waved and everyone laughed.

And then Dana saw her son Ax. She always watched her children, trying to find the bridge between them and her. This may be unnatural for a mother, she felt it was unnatural, but then it was unnatural to leave for seven years and lose the relationship of mother and child that should be hers. It should be her arms the children come to and her breasts they lay their head upon, but it wasn't. Especially at home she was cognizant of what she had lost and wanted so desperately to regain. It was a right that she had earned and never expected to sacrifice. It was a sacrifice foisted on her by poverty. She never spoke of it, but the anger at her choice, of poverty or isolation, burned a slow and steady burn. Never again would she leave her children, so poverty was their curse. This was her story. A story she repeated often in her mind.

Ax was taking a bath at the outside faucet. Which was unusual for anyone but Ax who was constantly finding a reason to wash.

"What is he taking a bath for now?" Dana asked Uncle Alex.

"I told him he smelled like an eel." It was a joke, something the family was always doing, but Ax took a bath immediately.

"Oh, don't encourage him."

"I wanted to smell like a jacket. I wanted to smell good," said Ax.

"Hey go get the garbage out, Ax," said his uncle, "so when the typhoon comes it will be clean."

"Give me five pesos."

Dana watched and listened to them laugh and crack jokes and laugh some more. They were hugging, wrestling.

Dana boiled some porridge and the children ate an afternoon snack. Everyone slept. At six o'clock Dana could feel the wind. It was not strong, but still pushed at the door.

Allan was saying, "It is coming. Are you sure you want to go on duty?"

When Dana left home for her twelve-hour nursing shift at the Lay's she was not sure how to explain her feelings. She did not cry. She was riding a public vehicle, but she felt like crying and even felt she was, on the inside.

When she had left the house everyone had stared, her mother-in-law and others. It seemed surreal. It was too much, this build-up to the storm and this leaving. She had hugged and kissed all the children, but Ax, always Ax had pulled away. And Allan, he was so intelligent, but unlucky in work. She trusted him with the children. He wasn't like his siblings, who were content to just survive at mother's house. He wanted more, for the children, for her and even for his fellow Filipinos. He was one of these people who don't fit into a subservient society. And she didn't either. Yet here they were.

Allan called.

"Do you want me to come home?" she asked

"No take care of your patient," he answered.

"Are you afraid?"

"Yes, but we can do it."

They hung up after this and Dana thought. "Yes we can do this." She rang the doorbell of the Lay family home. The two nurses she was replacing were waiting. They told her they would see her in the morning, before Typhoon Yolanda. She walked in and shut the door to the home and to her sadness.

Nelo teaches ballroom dancing in Manila. He was in Manila during Typhoon Yolanda dancing a slow swing with a rich girl. The music was sweet and the palms were swaying in the breeze from a storm far away. In Tacloban his wife and nine-year-old daughter were in his sister's house. The roof was gone and the marsh had become an ocean. The metal rolling shutters that covered the large spacious windows had been ripped away. His child and sister-in-law ventured downstairs, stepping to the wind and the music they could not hear. The child was first, leading, the sister-in-law above watching. The storm surge came and the sister-in-law darted back the way she had come leaving the child frozen on the last stair.

—From an aid worker's journal, 2014, Tacloban, Philippines

CHAPTER 3

The Roaring and The Waves

SAMUEL MAGDUA

At 3:00 am Samuel awoke. Geraldine and Sheila Mae were sleeping. The wind was beginning to pick up, but it was intermittent. He slipped from his bed and turned on the TV, GMA-7, channel ten. He watched the latest news on the storm, news that had been on all night. There was no blackout and he watched the reports for two hours until his brother Henry arrived from the Bureau of Fire Protection Agency. Henry had been on standby waiting for instructions at the city building. At the city building he had spent his time worrying about his family. His home was next to Samuel's. He finally had had enough of waiting. And though the wind was too strong to ride a motorcycle and the roads were thick with water, he found a way.

Samuel watched Henry ride in. He watched him go directly to his roof and began tying it down. Samuel did not bother to help. The wind was too strong and it had changed. He felt deep inside that something was different. He wasn't sure yet what was happening, but as the wind changed he remembered long before his father telling him about a Kabungan, the most dangerous of all winds. The Kanaway wind had joined the Amihan turning it into a typhoon. This he knew.

And then the Pumaga wind had turned it again, neutralizing it into a Salatran wind, a north wind. This was a normal event and diffused the typhoons. But this was no longer a Salatran. This was different. It was a wind to be feared, a wind to overrun all winds, a wind that has intelligence, a wind with a mind of its own. It tore through their village seeking out the lives and buildings it could destroy, a roaring, raging, conqueror.

This was the Kabungan wind, a wind from the South that travels north. In the course of an hour the Kabungan wind overran the Salatran and in the course of that hour the Kabungan began to lift roofs and shatter windows. Neighbors began to flee, searching for stronger shelter. The Biong family of five, Samuel's brother Ronaldo, Ronaldo's wife and the Bernabe couple found temporary refuge in Samuel's home. The metal on his roof was banging, the blocks holding them down were shaking and dancing on the tin. It seemed to Samuel that the Kabungan had brought chaos inside and out. Everyone around him was crying, screaming and yelling.

One of them was shouting over and over, "Oh my God we are all going to die. Oh my God!"

"Don't panic, don't panic." Samuel thought, but it was useless to shout over the wind and the people.

He picked up Sheila Mae and led the way toward brother Ramil's home on the bay. This was something Samuel and Ramil had talked about earlier in the day. Ramil's house was the best built home in the village. It was sandwiched between the bay and the ocean. It was twenty feet from Cancabato Bay at high tide and seven hundred meters from the Leyte Gulf.

Samuel did not run a straight path. The wind was pushing him from side to side, back and forth. A Kanbungan wind is a destructive wind. He knew the winds from a lifetime on the sea, but this wind he knew only from his father's stories. As he ran the wind was blowing apart the village. One by one the cement homes were coming down. Samuel, one of the oldest "tough guys" of the village began to cry. He clutched his daughter and could not see a place to run. He could not open his eyes in the wind. It was foggy with bullets of water. He could not see his wife, Geraldine. He could see no one. The wind was screaming, whistling, roaring, like a jet plane.

Samuel's run to Ramil's home was a treacherous dash for survival through a sea of shrapnel. Those following were not the only ones making that run. All around him people he could not see or hear were dashing for places that they perceived to be safe or safer than the shelters blowing up around them. Some didn't make it, some made it injured, but in Samuel's barangay almost everyone ran these gauntlets through crumbling shelters. At Samuel's brother's home, which seemed then a precarious location, thirty people found shelter. The last to arrive were not Samuel and his wife and the nine with them, but his brother Henry, Henry's wife and five children. The roof Henry had been tying down had taken off like a kite across the bay. By the time Henry arrived the door to Ramil's house was locked by the wind, as if nailed. Henry, like his brother Samuel, was immensely strong and with his five children and wife at risk he smashed through the door to safety. The wind followed him, pushing people about like police with clubs till they huddled terrified, cowering against the shaking walls and each other.

Thirty people, some strangers, took shelter inside, but Samuel huddled outside on the bay side, protected from the wind by the block wall and the comfort room, a small corner of refuge. He stayed outside to monitor the storm and give warning to Geraldine, Sheila Mae and the others just inside. Above him was a small blown out window. He chose to stay outside and watch the winds. It was safer inside, but he felt safer outside.

Samuel called on the most powerful One, but he did not yell at the storm as he had yelled at Ondoy. He did not challenge it as he had challenged Pablo. The Kabungan wind had taken away his voice and his strength. Samuel watched with disconnected eyes. He watched as the bay receded in front of him, sucked back like a huge vacuum exposing Lusay, a plant from the sea bottom. Plants that he should not see he was seeing. And then he found his voice again. He began to shout and scream at those inside.

"Get out!" he screamed. "The water is coming, get out!"

And it came back, black and silty, rolling over and over like a barrel. It was a whirlpool, opposite of a tornado, pulling down and in and when it hit the receded land it began to churn in a mad and violent boil. It was water you could not swim in. If it caught you, you should die. And it caught them all, in various stages of evacuation. In some miraculous fashion the thirty found their way dripping and torn, onto the metal roof. Samuel remembered bumping the roof overhang with his body and climbing on the tin. He does not remember pulling people out the broken window, tossing them up on the sheeting to safety. One after another he wrestled them as he had wrestled fish in a net, rocking violently in the mad surf. Henry later recalled that Samuel had pitched him like an old pillow. This Samuel did, but does not remember.

He does remember crouching with Geraldine and Sheila May, his brothers, sisters, nieces, nephews and seven strangers, men who had found their way to this piece of roof, that was a raft on a wall.

When the bay charged back to retake the land it had given up, sweeping back like a hoard of shaking hoofs and horns, it was met by the storm surge from the Pacific, sweeping across the seven hundred -meter peninsula as if it was a sprit of sand. The dead word—storm surge—that no one understood came alive. The water from the bay and the water from the Pacific, boiling and angry, met and stood and rose up in a tumultuous struggle. Samuel who clung to the metal roof on the peak that barely rose above the rushing water, but far below the crest, did not understand this other wave, or even the first wave. He watched, like a child, one fisherman's hand gripping the sharp tin, the other holding his daughter.

The surge from the Pacific continued on, like a conquering army, past them to Tacloban, to the Astrodome, to the Coke plant. It carried off Barangay 88, but it also carried other barangays too. Not far away in the blackness of the deep storm an old man named Carlito and his wife whirled past, hanging to the floor of a house.

At some point a young boy swept toward the roof, swirling like a banana leaf in the water. Samuel's twenty-year-old niece was clutching him around the neck, wrapping herself like a wet sheet around his chest and stomach. He still held Sheila May and Geraldine and was clutching the tin, yet somehow he managed to grab the boy's hand bobbing up and down in the water. He flung him to safety.

The boy lay on the roof and the men and women around him recoiled at the sight as he was limp and lifeless. "Resuscitate him!" he yelled at his brother Henry.

But Henry was afraid of the drowned boy. "No, No, I shouldn't touch him. He's dead. He's dead!"

"Resuscitate him, save him!"

"He has bubbles. He has bubbles in his mouth."

Samuel watched helplessly as the boy lay dying. He was grasped on all sides, yet he felt alone and helpless on the roof, while the boy lay unattended, bubbles of blood slipping out his lips and disappearing, like rose-colored balloons, in the wind.

Samuel and the others stayed on Ramil's roof for over two hours. They were buffeted by everything Yolanda could throw at them and yet they had held on and the roof on which they sat stayed too. The roof was detached and yet it did not wash or blow away. It stayed tethered on the walls as if it were one of their boats tethered to a rock on the shore. The thirty called on the powerful One. And when the water flowed back from where it had come they climbed exhausted off the roof and the roof too was tired. It slowly, gently eased its way off its perch and leaned up against a wall of the house. The drowned boy, half naked, grey and cold, clung as if still alive to the tin, and then his small hands let go and he slid roughly down.

Samuel had no words. No one had anything to say. The roof had become a lean-to and everyone, even the strangers, stayed under the makeshift shelter. They could see no neighbors. Nothing moved. Samuel thought that they were the only people who had survived. There were many dead bodies. There were three dead bodies that had washed into the house through the broken door and window. The walls had caught these corpses and the mud with them. It was hard to tell the difference. A month-old child lay dead on their roof; they did not know who she was or how she had gotten there. When the roof slid down the child stuck there like a wet grey rag. Samuel covered the dead boy's body with a muddy linen. He pulled the baby girl from the tin and covered her too.

At 4:00 pm Friday afternoon some of the thirty began to move around. They stepped tentatively out from under their makeshift tent and began to pick through the debris. There was no place to walk. Bodies and refuse were intermingled together. The dead were so thickly coated with black mud it was hard to make out, but Samuel counted fifty and then he stopped counting.

One of the strangers, a man who had survived on the roof with Samuel left the shelter and was climbing around the debris. He was sobbing and crying out to God, petitioning God for his family. His shouts disturbed the silence of Barangay 88 and other cries began to ring out. Twenty-two thousand people, less the few thousand who had left, and the thousands who lay dead, rose out of the rubble. In their rising they shouted for family and friends. They stared at the wounded and fractured bodies still living. They pleaded for help. A slow exodus began. It started with a hundred and swelled to thousands—men, women and children, old and young, making their way off this washed-out peninsula, down the Daniel Z. Romualdez Highway toward Tacloban.

A neighboring family was shouting for their son Angelo. They had four children, Adam, Eve, Angelo (named for Angel) and Algeorge—named for America's vice-president Al Gore and President George Bush—a conflicted name, as Algeorge was conceived unexpectedly, and unwanted. America, a foreign conqueror, always a part of this people, in governance, in education, and in names, was needed now. The neighboring family called out to God and America too.

Samuel and his brothers looked for food and looked for shelter, because that, is what survivors do. Samuel did not understand what had happened. He knew that the roof of his brother's house should not have stayed—no other roofs stayed—or the walls of the house that supported them should not have stood, no other walls were standing. He could not explain his survival. He could not explain the winds or the waves. For the most part his neighbors had not survived. Later San Jose came up with a word for families that all died. They called it wholesale. There was a lot of wholesale in Barangay 88.

One blanket had black thick locks that flowed out from under it like blood. Nelo lifted the blanket, and the camera looked into the face of his child. The camera did not stop looking. It recorded him speaking to his child for a long time, covering and uncovering her body—fingering her single headband, jeweled and curved like a snake—but the camera did not record his voice, just the image of his hand and her body, quiet and peaceful.

—From an aid worker's journal, 2014, Tacloban, Philippines

C H A P T E R   3

The Roaring and The Waves

NOEL LITO

N oel woke up at 5:00 am Friday morning. The dark cell window that was open to the outside—just bars, no glass—had come alive. The wind was bursting through the opening and running about the cell looking wildly for a place to land. The forty-three men were all awake. Some were sitting on the floor. Many were praying. Noel was not worried about himself. None of the prisoners were worried about themselves. They prayed for their families who were living in the squatter homes of Tacloban. Hundreds of homes are built in the bay on wooden poles pounded by hand into the sea bottom. The homes are connected by a maze of docks and walkways, where children run on sunny days and leap naked into the water. Noel had grown up on these docks.

This was the city jail after all, not the provincial prison, where the convicted are transferred. All of them had families in Tacloban. Noel worried for his relatives. The wind seemed too big for such a small window. There was apprehension in the room, and the prisoners, including Noel, turned their worry into silent prayer or just silence. For an hour they sat in their cell or stood along the walls saying nothing, just praying.

The prison began to shake, the massive stone and steel structure shuddering in the wind. Noel heard the scraping and tearing of metal as the roof began to tear off. The sound of the storm was oppressive, magnified by the fearful hush of his cellmates. The only noise was the wind's many hands ripping and tearing off metal and all the while spinning around the cell, angrier and angrier.

Noel saw one of the leaders of his gang, the Batang Samar Leyte Gang at the door of his cell and then it was open. The gang leader had a key to the BSL cells and the women's cells. Noel and his cellmates moved out into the courtyard. They moved out without pushing or shoving, like ducks in a line. Debris was flying everywhere. The convicts in the Batang City Jail Gang saw them out there and began to call for help. They shouted and screamed at their fellow prisoners. Noel looked at them dumbly and then he scurried to the wall and buried himself against it. There was no place to go.

The courtyard was submersed almost as soon as Noel was released from his cell. The water poured through the barred windows like over a dam. It was black muddy water that flushed out the last of the men, pushing them into the commons and then filling the courtyard like a tub.

Noel found himself struggling in the courtyard. He gulped quantities of water and battled the swirling torrent to keep from drowning. Someone from the second floor began to throw empty five-gallon water jugs to them. He grabbed one. The men who had made it to the second floor were emptying water jugs, capping them and throwing them down. Desperate men grabbed these jugs.

The women were shouting, the men in the BGG cells were screaming to be let out.

Noel did not shout. Soundlessly in his heart and mind he cried out to God. His mind recited a mumbled incoherent rosary. He thought what he was taught to think. His body fought to survive. Noel became two men, one embracing the teachings he knew of God, which were submissive and traditional and one resisting the forces around him, which were frantic and transforming. These two men were separated by a great chasm in the storm. The chasm always existed. The storm enhanced their realities. Noel did not feel incarcerated in the typhoon surge. He felt physically liberated, yet it was a liberation of muscles, sinews, and lungs. If he had thought, if he was one man, he may have drowned.

The prisoners in the BGG cells had torn off the exhaust vents in the ceiling and were escaping through the openings. The roof was gone and they were going too. There were many guards on duty, but between the wind and the water the prison had become a massive trap, and even the free men sought escape from the clutches of the wind and the waves.

The water continued to rush in, spilling over the cement walls. Noel held his water jug. Then he lost it. Someone tore it from his hands. He rocked from side to side, bumping into other men. He grabbed the back of someone, felt the wet skin and bones of the man's shoulders and then a hand pried him off, short strong fingers pressing into his own, squeezing until his knuckles cracked and Noel soundlessly let go. The courtyard was just a mass of men, women, black water and wind that moaned with the sorrow of Christ Himself. The water was being stirred, as if two great hands were washing themselves, churning up a putrid black mud. Noel sucked in giant draughts of sodden air, mixed with the dirt of these great hands and was surprised to taste the salt of the ocean. He remembered his days as a boy running and jumping in the sea. It seemed he was there again, swimming under the homes on stilts, bumping up against the poles and scraped by the current, holding his breath until his head was light and airy. He tried to swim. He tried to breathe. He saw a bottle in the wind, falling like a leaf on a windy day. It had come from the far side of the prison courtyard on the second floor and it weaved and floated in the air across the fifty meters until it cracked him on the side of his face. He grasped it and rode it until it carried him to a second floor ladder. Strong hands pulled him up and out of the surge. He lay silently on the concrete walkway. Time became the storm itself and blended together for him. He does not remember either well.

Two months after the storm we met Nelo at his sister's house where his daughter died. He told us, "When the dogs howl I hear my daughter." He would like to leave this house. He has been eating only white bread and drinking warm Coke from a two-liter bottle. He has been here for seven weeks, keeping guard.

He offered us his bread. There were five dirty slices wrapped in plastic, with a frosting of green mold on one piece.

"Thank you," we said and brought him to the Palami home where he piled his plate with rice and chicken adobe, vegetables, and after his cigarette he had flan that I had found earlier that day in the market.

He left then and went back to his sister's home and the ghost of his daughter. He wears a camouflage hat and dark glasses and stands in the shell of his bedroom window with smoke curling around his head, to scare off the looters.

—From an aid worker's journal, 2014, Tacloban, Philippines

C H A P T E R   3

The Roaring and The Waves

ALLAN LABITA

Allan was up on and off all night. He sent out text messages to people in different parts of the province, trying to monitor the storm and the progress. At 4:00 am his friend Boyen called unexpectedly from Barugo, which is fifty kilometers south of Tacloban.

"It is already in Guiuan (Guiuan is 154 km east of Tacloban), evacuate, evacuate. It will hit by 5:00 am. You had better go. I will call you later."

Allan was not sure where Boyen had gotten his information, but he knew Boyen had a connection with someone in Manila. The wind began to pick up and blow harder, but in ebbs and flows. He adjusted the volume of the radio to a higher setting so he could monitor the storm's progress over the sound. Allan woke his brothers to inform them of the landfall in Guiuan and the rising wind. He called Dana to let her know the Typhoon was coming sooner than expected.

"Okay," she said. "Keep the kids and everyone safe."

"Yes," Allan replied.

He called his sister Agnes in Biliran to warn them. They were one hundred kilometers west, but in the storm's direct path.

Allan and his brothers went over to their uncle's house. At their uncle's Allan woke everybody up and told them about the new developments. Allan had the children who were sleeping get up and put on shoes.

"Why dad?"

"Because there might be glass. I am wearing shoes so you use shoes."

Allan went back to his house and his mother followed him. He wanted to take care of any final details. He ran around unplugging cords and putting last minute things in place and on shelves in case of flooding. The wind had picked up and the metal roof was banging, making noises like gunshots. He came out of his room closing the door behind him. Kim and Arman had come over to get mother. They were telling her to end her morning prayers. She was ignoring them, sitting in her easy chair, continuing the rosary, oblivious to their presence.

The radio was on and Allan went over and put his ear by it one last time. It was a field broadcast. The reporter did not seem sure about the typhoon, whether it was making landfall or this strong wind was just a pre-warning and it was still journeying toward Samar. He seemed frantic, shouting into the receiver, "The typhoon is increasing. The winds are exceeding 300 kilometers. Everyone on the coastal area must evacuate…"

Next-door Allan's sisters were screaming at everyone to get out of the house and over to the uncles.

"Allan! Get Nanay (grandmother), Kim and Arman, the roof, get out!"

Allan told his brothers to go back to their uncle's and that he would bring his mother over. For the next hour Allan struggled to get his mother to return to his uncle's house. The wind was steadily increasing, the rain was torrential and it was slowly eating into the roof of their home. His mother was fearful and stubborn, determined to trust her saints. Allan felt incredibly trapped between the respect and due he must pay his mother and her faith, which was his heritage too and a typhoon that had become a life and death struggle. Between the mother and son raged this eternal conflict, he shouting, cajoling and pleading to get his mother to leave her house and her saints, while she sat immobile and silent except for the murmuring and fumbling of the rosary.

"Oh my god, Mom, do not do this," he shouted.

"It is not fair to us. Everyone has left. Don't put me in this hard situation. Don't put me in danger. Oh my god. What is the point? What do you want? What is the reason? Which one, okay, what do you want?"

She was holding a bible.

"Anything else?"

She wanted five saints transferred to higher shelves. Allan without a word put the Black Nazarene, the Jesus Christ, the Mama Mary, and the Santo Niño to where she motioned.

Finally she was ready and she struggled out of the easy chair and on her feet to the door. There were no winners, there was no peace. The structure of their house was shaking. The wind was deafening with a whistling sound and the sheathing on the roof was impatient, wanting to be unfettered from the nails. It was 5:55 am in the morning. At some point the radio stopped, though Allan did not notice. The storm raged inside him as well as out. Foremost he was a father and the religion of his mother had interceded, keeping his children parentless next door.

They stumbled toward their uncle's house. He held the fifth statue, St. Anthony of Padua, in his arms. His mother had her bible and St. Santo Niño. They walked slowly, bent over, Allan just behind his mother, shuffling his feet so as to not run her over, yet wanting to run and needing to run. The rain was not rain, but a wild salty spray, terribly strong.

Debris was being thrown from the houses surrounding them. The sky was full of fragments. He thought of Dana and his children. He did not feel afraid.

He walked into his uncle's house and it was if he had been gone a year. The children were cowering and motionless like statues. Everyone looked wide-eyed and in shock. Ax sat huddled in a corner covering his ears. His mother was wailing as she entered. Aileen's mouth was moving and she was shouting. The roof of their uncle's house was banging.

When Allan walked into his uncle's house and looked at the frozen faces of the adults, the terrified eyes of his four children and his seventeen-year-old niece sitting immobile on the scattered array of chairs and sofa he felt oddly energized, even angry. Not angry at anyone or even anything, but the circumstances galvanized him and he felt violently protective. He grabbed a chair and broke the window, smashing the glass and hammering the shards from the sill. He looked at his brothers and Uncle Alex, none of whom were moving, frozen in terror. The wind was moaning, giving birth to fear and hopelessness. The people trapped in Yolanda were held first by the wind. It was like an animal, captivating them by its other-worldly force and its cry, a guttural wail. Only a few, such as Allan, were able to block out the storm's paralytic power.

"Everyone get a child!" he said and then he repeated it again to each of them face to face, screaming inches from their faces. "Everyone get a child! We are going to transfer to the yellow house!"

Adjacent to Allan's uncle's house was a two story yellow house. Allan and his uncle had decided that if they needed to move because of flooding the yellow house would be safer, evacuation plans they had discussed with the owners of the yellow house, though no one expected to need them. "Everyone must carry a child."

The adults began to respond. They began to mill around and gather a child, except mother who grasped her saint, rocking back and forth, moaning like the wind, but soundless, just her mouth opening and closing. As Allan bawled to them from the window the first of the water came boiling into the house, black and ankle deep. Outside the road, lined with houses and concrete fences and metal gates, had become a raging river.

Arnel was the first out and he carried Allan's youngest daughter Bridgette. Allan was second with Coleen. Before he went through the window he looked at the faces, Aileen terrified, his mother squeezing the life from her saint, the boys following, Uncle Alex looking old and lined. "Be quick!" he shouted. "Stay on track!"

And as planned they crawled out the window one by one. Uncle Alex carried Ax, Phill was with Kim, Yugi was with Arman, and then the women and it seemed to Allan that everyone was out. They were bunched on the concrete veranda, the water was knee deep and swirling, the wind a feral animal screaming and tearing at their clothes and skin.

Allan pushed Coleen into Armida's arms and went to the corner of the house. "Now! He screamed. "Now…." But the water, which submerged him, muffled his words. It was pitch black and thick and boiling. It washed him against his neighbor's wall and held him down for what seemed forever. It tore at him, like huge mauling hands, ripping at his clothes, pulling off his shoes, grabbing out his dentures, suffocating him. He struggled and fought in a helpless dance, his limbs rushing through the water, like minnows on a string. He was dragged to the street and the corner of his neighbor's and Uncle Alex's small courtyard, where the building, like a big arm, grabbed him. He crawled up and on the shed roof of the yellow house. There he witnessed Yolanda's fury. A fifteen foot surge, he knew the name now, was around them, crashing into every structure still standing, twisting and turning homes into rubble.

"Oh my god," he said. "Where did everyone go?" From Allan's vantage point on this metal roof he could on a clear day see his uncle's courtyard and house and the whole of his street down to the Daniel Z. Romualdez Highway snaking its way to the airport. He would also have seen a community of tin roofs, colorful with clothes drying, or speckled with tires and blocks to hold them to makeshift walls. But during Yolanda, with the wind exceeding two hundred and fifty kilometers an hour, he could barely open his eyes. The water, full of horrifying gods, raged around him. The wind in labor screamed and he too screamed, blind and agonized.

He saw Arnel like a ghost through the wind. Arnel was hanging on the power line and Allan's six-year-old Bridgette was with him. Bridgette did not seem like a ghost, her face was clear, her eyes were big. He could see her clearly.

"Hold on! I'm coming to get you!" No one answered. He screamed to himself and to the wind, and to God who was there too.

Allan clung on the side of the roof, which wasn't a roof now, just a wall with tangled metal rafters and joists and pulled in Bridgette, who gripped him, clawing him. He saw Arman climbing up on the roof. Yugi was not with him.

He watched Arnel on the wire. "Hang on Bro," he shouted. "Hang on."

And to Arman he shouted. "Get up. Quick. Get yourself to that window." And he pointed to the yellow house side window.

Arnel was holding the power line with two hands. The water tugged and pulled at him, kicking him about. "Hang on Bro," Allan shouted again.

He turned to Arman and saw another man climbing up to the window where Arman was just huddled. It was Kim pushing up Allan's eldest son Phill. Phill was crying. The two of them, Arman and Phill sat outside the yellow house window, vulnerable to the wind.

"Stop crying Phill, I'm going to get you. Hang on tight."

And then to Arman he said, "Find your way in, so you can get Phill."

And to Kim, "Climb quick and help Arman."

Just that suddenly the water had spit the brothers up and out. Allan, Kim, Arman on the roof, Arnel dangling from the power line, and with them, two of his four children, Allan with Bridgette and Phill with Kim. Allan watched Arman by the window of the yellow house, not moving. He screamed at him again. "Find a hard object. Break the glass... quick. *Tol*," which was a name Allan used for him.

In the yellow house the people were not moving either. They were crouched across from the window staring blankly and fearful, not seeing the shadows of Allan's brothers there. When Arman broke the window, smashing it in with a piece of debris, they still did not move, just sat there. Kim and Phill went in and so did Arman.

"Get back out the window." Allan screamed to them. "I am going to get Bridgette to you. Get a grip on the steel frame."

He fought the wind and the twisted steel of the window and pried Bridgette off him. He handed her to Kim, and then back again he went, along the wall to the street where Arnel hung on the wire. The water was twisting and turning Arnel like a wrestler, wearing him down, not pinning him, but pointing him to death. The wind was pushing Allan too, but it did not scrape him off the roof and it did not frighten him. Allan had entered a different world. A place where men dream of going in times such as these, but rarely do. A place where fear is silenced, pain is disregarded and action is a gift packed like dynamite into a human's body, powerful, explosive, and alive. He began to talk to the wind, but he did not yell or shout at it. In its fury he lost and found himself.

He watched Arnel on the wire and his brother's face looked gentle and feminine. It was like his features had softened, as if he was holding his baby niece on the sofa in their house. Arnel held his niece on the wire in the midst of Yolanda's fury. There was peace, a sweet peace. Allan moved to Arnel, hoping to save him, but he didn't save him. Yugi, Allan's son, saved him. Yugi came out of the water and floated, bobbing like a cork to the electric line, which Arnel still grasped.

"Hold on Yugi! I will get you! *Brod*. Hold on Yugi, I'm going to pull you both up." Allan was crying and he was rushing to them.

Arnel looked at him blankly, softly, his hands slipping.

"*Brod*! No, no, no, no!" And then Arnel heard Allan and he extended his hand to Yugi and gripped the line.

Together Allan and Arnel pulled in Yugi and then one by one family members began to emerge and were pulled to the roof, Tina first, then Armida, *Tiya* Nene (Allan's aunt), Sing-Sing, *Tiya's* seventeen-year-old niece and finally Arnel left his wire and was helped to the roof.

Uncle Alex, Aileen, Coleen, *Nanay* (mother) and Ax did not surface. Allan did not feel hopeless. He grabbed a two-by-four and broke open the ceiling of his uncle's house to see if anyone was still there. He peered in and watched the water.

Allan alone stayed on the rafters. He did not feel the wind, though it had not abated. He heard Tata Leo calling out his name and asking for help. Tata Leo was a neighbor who lived on the far side of his mother's house. Allan crossed his uncle's home, stepping through the rafters, traversing his mother's home, which too was just rafters, to Tata Leo's family of ten, hiding in their ceiling, between the wind and water. One by one Allan transferred them to the yellow house. Ten souls and then two more "strangers" hanging on to some cables. He got them all. He carried them all. One by one across the rafters of broken homes he carried them to the yellow house, through the window to safety.

He was the last to crawl in. There were thirty-one people there. Everyone in the house was crying, except his sister Tina. She was looking at Allan and silently she was asking. "Where are the others?" Allan looked from face to face, but he knew all who were missing. He felt powerless, human and weak. Like the others he huddled, while the wind tore the houses and trees around them, feeding them to the water, which beat it all into a black porridge of debris.

At 9:00 am the water receded to five feet, fighting its way back to the ocean almost as fiercely as it had come, sucking away anything it could grab. Kim was the first to see Aileen. She was lying on the wreckage of a building ten meters from the window of the yellow house.

Without a word, Allan went out, down the stairs, making for the front door, but the swirling water in the first floor stopped him and he went back upstairs to the window, to the roof and jumped in unthinking. He struggled to swim to Aileen, but the water's current pushed him away. He fought his way back to the roof. Arman had a curtain rope and tied it around Allan's waist. He jumped in again, fighting against an ocean that was in a desperate retreat to its home two kilometers away. Again Allan could not reach Aileen.

"Pull me in." He shouted.

He went in one last time without the curtain rope and this time he reached her. She was limp, like a soft doll. Yolanda had taken all her clothes but a pair of light yellow panties. He dragged her through the water to the house and up the stairs. He pumped her chest and tried to start her heart. He tried to resuscitate her. Only bubbles came out of her mouth and they mixed with his tears.

"I love you, I love you," was all he could speak, and he spoke that over and over. And as he worked over a dead Aileen, the water left as quickly as it had come, pulling his drowned neighbors to the ocean shore, where it deposited them like alewives on the mangled beaches. The family of the yellow house, Tata Leo's ten, the two strangers, Allan's brothers and sisters, and his own children watched Allan cry and work over his sister's naked body. They were bystanders, as silent and motionless as Aileen, unconsciously trying to protect their minds for the future, blocking out the images of Aileen's bloated and blue body, of Allan, dirty, wet, broken and of the ones that weren't there. It was 9:30 am Friday morning.

When Typhoon Yolanda came as a raging force of nature, it tore the natural to pieces, but that in itself was not the horror. This keeps coming back to me that typhoons are incredible forces of nature and of earth, but they are not horrible. It is man's involvement, man's passing that makes them so.
  —From an aid worker's journal, 2014, Tacloban, Philippines

CHAPTER 3

The Roaring and The Waves

DOLOR LINGO

Dolor and Dante woke up at 5:00 am. Their house, always a refuge, was creaking in the wind. Dolor shook out the blankets and folded them. Dante stepped outside to observe the weather. He ran down the alley across the street past mother's house to check on the waves.

Minutes later he returned. "The waves are huge…. The winds, the winds are very strong. I think they are increasing."

Their house, a place where typhoons could not reach, was shaking and the roof was pulling against the ropes, ropes that Dolor thought hours before were unnecessary.

"Lord!" Dolor cried. "You must stop the wind. It is so strong."

"I want to be with the children. Let's go to your mothers."

"Go," I will come as soon as I put away these things.

Dante left, venturing out into the wind to Dolor's mothers and the children. Dolor stayed and folded and stored the mats. She put the TV and oven roaster on the floor. She sat on one of the chairs, praying and praising God together, pleading to Him to calm the winds and to calm her. She was scared. The wind and the rain were as one. She could see the wind moving, like a live writhing beast. Coconut trees were being uprooted. A pedicab went running past with no driver. The neighbor's house started to collapse in the wind.

The wind bit and stung her as she ran. She curled her hands over her head and ran a gauntlet of debris, fighting through everything Yolanda could throw at her, rushing to her mother's.

"Lord save them," Dolor said to herself. "Lord save them."

There were eighteen people at Dolor's mother's house—the big house—with Dante and Dolor. Dolor's brother, who would have made it nineteen, had left thirty minutes before. The big house was solidly built with one meter by one-meter foundations. The beams were one foot by one-foot reinforced concrete. The rafters were steel, as was the roof. It had a painted plywood ceiling.

When Dolor arrived everyone was up and huddled in the back kitchen and bedroom area. There was no shouting. The children were silent. No one was crying. The waves and wind had joined and it was if the house was being fired on by cannons. The blows were jolting the big house.

Dante gathered his children in his arms. He pushed all four in a tight circle and squeezed. Dolor laid her hands on them and thanked God for safety. She was so glad to be with them, so glad to be together.

Little by little the water began to come into the big house. First it was ankle deep, then knee deep, and then waist and chest deep. It kept rising, pushing its way in and it was like someone had a big spoon and the house was a pot and everything was swirling around.

Dante, the only man, tore out the plywood ceiling in the kitchen and one by one he boosted the twelve children into the rafters and out of the water.

"Do not leave Carl," Dante told his oldest, thirteen-year-old Daniel. Carl was their third son, seven years old.

Then the water was above the ceiling and Dolor was trapped. She fought to get through the quarter inch plywood ceiling. She clawed at it with her fingers, hitting it until she broke through, gasping for breath. She bobbed up and down in the splintered opening, holding a rafter near the wall. She saw other heads bobbing too. The children were tucked up into the peak. The roof was still on.

The children overwhelmed Dante. Dolor's mother and Aunt Jane were older and helpless, so that left Dolor, her two sisters and himself. As Dolor fought to break through the plywood ceiling, Dante had only eyes for the children. On the first wave he had gotten them in the ceiling. When the second wave came Dante pushed the children onto the concrete beams, tucking them below the steel roof. He did not shout or cry out. The time had passed for that. He could hear nothing but the wind. The water tried to thwart him, like a gang of thugs in a narrow alley. He pushed through it, took its beatings and got—he thought—the children to safety.

The second wave submerged Dolor. She was hitting her head on the pitched roof. She dove down into the black water, feeling with her hands for the window. Somehow she opened the window and climbed out. She came out of the water and clung to the roof, gripping a piece of sheeting with both hands. The sheeting was alive in her fingers. The wind was breathing life into it and eventually it flew, like a tailless kite swooping up and down and over and back again to earth, which was now an ocean. When the sheeting hit the water Dolor let go.

The wind sounded like a plane taking off. There was a punching sound, like a hammer beating a loose board and a booming whistle. It was a cauldron of noise all mixed together. Dolor started to swim. And whether she had flown seventy meters, or somehow been swept over the houses and factory she did not know, because she was in back of the Hot Chile factory.

Dolor just kept swimming, dragging herself out of the whirlpools, fighting to get to a tree, any tree. She made it to a talisay tree. It was twelve inches in diameter with hard rough bark. The water was rolling up and down and swirling and so strong it spun Dolor with it. She was washed around and around the tree, till the flesh on her arms, chest and legs were blood red.

When the second wave came Dante transferred the children to the concrete beams, but this is all he could do. The wind was tearing at the roof. It was howling, it was beating the roof like a madman with a stick and a can. He did not see any of the women.

Dolor never saw the third wave. It towered over the big house and when it fell the house fell with it, exploding and crumbling, the thick footings sucked away like pebbles on the shore.

When the water began to recede Dolor was six meters up on the talisay tree. She had no idea where she was. The landscape was completely altered. What was green was brown, where once had stood a tropical forest, now were bare roots, like veins crawling from the soil. What had been homes were now slabs of concrete. Even the tree she hung on was broken above her, pinched off like a gardener pinches a flower off a stem.

Dolor climbed down and made her way, wading and swimming toward the Hot Chile building. The massive structure had disappeared. The shrimp pits were swirling with black sea water. The roof was gone. The walls and everything mounted on them were gone. One car had found its way into a pit and another rested precariously on the raised slab.

She met her husband Dante nearby. They embraced each other.

"Where are our children?"

"I do not know," he answered.

Men throwing ropes had pulled Dante, one of Dolor's sisters, a nephew and niece from the water.

"We must find our children." Yet as Dolor looked around, the landscape was not a land of life, but of death. Nothing was moving; the earth was a sodden still grey. She began to comprehend that there were no children. She did not second-guess. Her life was not so much a life of choices, but of fate. The Lingo's, more than most people, pursued life trusting in a frailty of faith. They worked more, served more, loved more and trusted more. And they accepted the result of their effort as ordained. Fairness mattered, as did corruption. But they did not question their circumstance. That would be tantamount to questioning God Himself.

In this case, fate intervened and they heard a child calling, "Mama, Mama, I am here."

It was twelve-year-old Dante, Junior.

Dolor's only thought was that if one was alive, then there was hope for the others. The three of them clung to each other as if by clinging they could grasp life from the death surrounding them. For a long time they held each other. She thanked God over and over and over. She thanked Him because that was all she was capable of doing. Her faith allowed her nothing more.

Hot Chile caretakers found the cold bodies of thirteen-year-old Daniel and seven-year-old David Carl at 10:00 am. A girder from Dolor's mother's house pinned them down. It lay across their stomachs. Before the children were hoisted into the ceiling, Dante had told Daniel, "Whatever you do, do not leave your brother Carl." When the boys were found they were still holding hands and that too was fate and a small measure of comfort. Daniel's cold body had a small scratch on the left side of his face. David was unmarked.

Saturday morning they found five-year-old Princess Diana. She was buried three meters from Dolor's talisay tree, as brown and grey as the surroundings. Two other family members were found there as well.

I woke up in the early morning, I had been dreaming and was in the back of a church with the pastor intoning the word death, over and over, in throaty raspy voice, but it wasn't the pastor it was just the neighbor's dog barking. I lay and listened to the dog and he was barking death in a throaty raspy bark over and over. I wasn't discomforted. The dream wasn't bad. Death was just a bark—the bark just a word.

—From an aid worker's journal, 2014, Tacloban, Philippines

CHAPTER 3

The Roaring and The Waves

CARLITO QUIAS

Claring and Carlito woke up together at 4:00 am Friday morning. The anger of the evening before still hung in the air. Claring began to clean the kettles, washing up the dishes and placing them in boxes. Carlito gathered the clothes that were on the line outside, folding and bagging them. There was no wind. Four o'clock was their normal wakeup time. They did not speak a word to each other. They silently went about the business of the morning, preparing for a typhoon.

Carlito stepped outside to observe the weather. He stayed outside for an hour, smoking his cigarettes, cupping them in his hand to light them. He did not think just about the typhoon, though the wind was steadily increasing. He was thinking more about the tension inside and how to survive it.

Shortly after five o'clock the mangoes began to blow off the trees. Carlito rushed around, like a squirrel, gathering them and piling them by the side of his house. This was an opportunity. Normally the mangoes would be shared in the community.

At 5:30 am Carlito went back inside and everyone was talking about transferring to the barangay hall across the street because

113

the wind was so strong. The barangay hall was a two story cement building fifty meters northwest across the DZR airport road. Different members of the family were gathering their belongings, but no one was sure what to do. The roof and house were shaking from the wind. Carlito did not look at his wife and she did not look at him.

At 6:00 am, Jun, who had left at 11:00 pm, arrived with two friends, Jomer and Erning, from the Astrodome. Willy, another son of Claring, who lived a few blocks away, joined them. All four had come to get the family to a safe place.

"I am okay here," stated Claring.

No one argued. "Okay, Mother," said Willy. "Edwin, and I will stay with you."

Carlito did not say anything; it was expected he would stay, and he stayed.

Carlito's son Rex and his pregnant wife Reah, Roning, Jun, Jomar, Erning, Friggy and five of the six children, all except baby Sunshine, left for the Barangay Hall. Carlito watched them go. He could only see them faintly, shadows in the storm. There were a lot of flying objects. Roofs were coming off. The ten were trying to take cover as they ran. Scurrying from place to place. He saw a piece of corrugated steel hit his daughter-in-law Reah in the leg and she stumbled on the roadway. Then the twelve were gone, blanketed by the wind.

Carlito watched them and his heart felt sickeningly heavy. It had been heavy before during the conflict with Claring, but now it felt too heavy for his body. Or maybe it was his body that felt light and wispy. He went and stood by Claring. He reached over and held her hand. He was holding it when the first wave came. The ten who were running to the barangay hall to safety disappeared in the black water of the ocean.

The four that were left with Carlito, Willy, Edwin, baby Sunshine, and Claring climbed out an opening of their roof to an adjacent two-story house next door. Carlito carried Sunshine. The five sat on the second floor of the adjacent home. None of them spoke. The second wave came. Carlito watched numbly as the houses around them were being washed away. They clustered there, holding to each other.

When the third wave came the five of them were still sitting on the second floor. The third wave was the last wave. The first had muddied them, the second had almost drowned them, the third destroyed what was left. The house they were on, like all the other houses, was floating. Carling told Carlito they had to hold on to each other and so they did, clutching the legs and arms and hands of each other in a mad quest for survival. The house disappeared beneath them and the second floor became a raft on the rushing water, churning like a washing machine, swirling and pushing, up, down, around. Carlito was hit on the head by a corrugated sheet of metal. The blood poured out. Debris cut his body.

The first of the five to vanish was Edwin. He was there and then he was gone. Carlito was holding on the edge of the raft on his knees and Sunshine lay between his legs. He pushed Sunshine over to Willy. Carlito's strong arms—with the tough sinews and strong muscles of hard labor—gripped and held on to the raft, like a vise, and he felt nothing at all. A few minutes later Willy and Sunshine were gone too.

Carlito's raft was swept across the peninsula, past the barangay hall where some of the family had set out to seek refuge, past Samuel Magdua, the fisherman, and the thirty or so people hanging on a tin roof. It was carried across Cancabato Bay toward the Coca Cola factory on the southwestern shore. In a matter of minutes it traveled four kilometers, bobbing and weaving like a drunken fighter and all the time Carlito did what he needed to do to save himself—he held on.

He was faintly aware that Claring was there too, but he did not acknowledge her or think about her. When the raft reached Burayan, the shoreline community near the Coca Cola plant it sank and Carlito and Claring were swimming. He paddled the water frantically, losing his prescription glasses. He remembered that later, those glasses. He had paid one thousand pesos for them. Claring gripped his arm and he thrashed with his other, trying to stay afloat in the whirlpool. For ten minutes or so the two of them swam together in a frenetic dance, clinging and fighting, sucking great draughts of the muddy water. They were very tired.

And then Claring let go. Her hand slipped off his arm with a tentative twitch, a soft caress. He did not reach out for her or grab her. He was trying to stay alive, flailing the water. She was a burden to let go and she must have realized that. He tried to look back to get a glimpse of her, but the water had sucked her like a vacuum and she was gone.

When Claring let go, disappearing into the surge, Carlito continued on in a desperate struggle of survival. There was little he could do. The water had a will of its own and he was pushed and twisted, bobbing like a jug of coconut wine, barely able to breathe, and then breathing salty thick air. He would have died, never again to finger a cigarette lovingly and feel the smoke soothe the agony of his past, the children he had left, the families he had abandoned, but he didn't die. Not yet.

A fifteen-year-old boy floated by him and the boy had a corked bottle he was hanging onto. He shared the jug and Carlito took it frantically, clutching on to its smooth sides with his strong sinewy fingers and forearms that had not lost their strength. This happened all over the city. The poor men—men who had spent a lifetime toiling, and in the process had honed their muscles to last hour after hour after hour—these men survived. It was the women and children who drowned, and if by chance a rich man was caught in the flood, he too fell short. When Yolanda brought the deprived and prosperous together like runners on a track—as if to test their life choices—it was the poor who ran stumbling forward while the rich just stumbled.

A young girl swirled by. She caught Carlito by the shirt and climbed on his back. She gripped him around the neck and held him, choking him. They fought on the bottle, both to survive, no anger involved, but wrestling uncontrollably. The fifteen-year-old boy watched. Carlito broke the girl's grip, transferred it to the bottle and he slipped off and away in the current. The two, boy and girl, were swept to a tree, which they grabbed and clung to, wrapping their bodies around it and around each other. Carlito saw their embrace.

He was alone in the black water, being swept toward a two-story house and a coconut tree that leaned against it. The closer he came to the house the faster the water seemed to race, like a plane landing, a raging buloso, the surroundings magnifying the speed. He grabbed the coconut tree, climbed on it and lay there. He lay there for two hours, though it felt like minutes, and then made his way up the trunk to the ceiling of the house. He crawled onto the ceiling joists. The water was slowly receding. He thought about Claring. He wanted to get home to Costa Bravo and to his house. He saw the boy and girl far off untangle themselves and climb down from the tree. He saw the light brighten, dim, go black and then he did not see anything for a long time.

I have a visitor. A young child from the village. They are happy we are here. The children have helped us gather shells. They played some football with us on the beach. I gave the children an apple and said one bite each. They gathered in a pack around that apple and slowly passed it from one to another, until just a piece of the core was left. This visitor of mine does not make a sound. He leans with one arm on my table, rocks back and forth, climbs here and there, and shuffles over to look across the woodless forest. He has few teeth. They are rotted in the front. Off he goes and leaps a log, then another, to the beach and beyond. I do not know his name. He is just a child, one of many.

—Visiting Samar, from an aid worker's journal, 2014, Tacloban, Philippines

C H A P T E R   3

The Roaring and The Waves

R E G I E   P A A

At 5:00 am Regie woke. He had to urinate, but didn't want to get up. He fell back asleep and woke again at six o'clock. Between five and six the wind had become livid. The Toyota Crosswind was rocking, banging against the car next in line, like it was being punched against the ropes, bouncing back and punched again. With every punch the new car became less new. Regie had to pry the door open to get out. He darted to the car Wendell was sleeping in, keeping low and trying to shelter himself from the rain and wind.

He pounded on the back window. "Get up Wendell," he shouted. "We have to go to Kuya Boy's." The wind took his words and tangled them like string. He saw that Wendell, who loved to sleep, was somehow still sleeping. He saw the blanket move and hand wave. The wind was whistling and the whistle turned to a wail. Regie ran to Kuya Boy's. He did not run to the display center office, because he did not think the coconut lumber office would hold up in the storm.

The rain was like needle pricks. He covered his face as he ran.

There were a total of six at Kuya Boy's house: Kuya Boy, his wife Ate Malyn and their children, Jude 19, Jocelyn 17, Abigail 14 and their 32 year old helper Bobby. Regie's arrival made seven. Regie kept looking out the window to see if Wendell was getting out. He had been in the first car and Wendell in the third and it seemed as if the five cars were in a queer dance, bumping and colliding with every howl of the wind.

When Wendell finally ran out of the car he was sleeping in, the water was knee deep. Regie watched his friend dash to the old vacant house nearest to the cars. The second wave came just after Wendell had fled. It lifted the cars like toys, collapsing the display center office and pushing the house Wendell had transferred to into Bobby the helper's house. The two old houses joined, as if at a marriage altar and the water swept them like dust from a broom toward Regie. Regie prayed for Wendell. He felt the shudder in Kuya Boy's thick walls as the two old homes collapsed and disintegrated against the solid walls.

The wind began to shatter the windows. Regie heard a hissing noise, as it created a crack and the panes would burst out, one after another, like a string of firecrackers. The wind was screaming. Water was squirting through the broken windows. Up to this point Kuya Boy had been telling everyone where to go, but the family and Bobbie were panicking, including Kuya Boy. The water in the house was three feet high. The seven of them waded into the comfort room and bolted the door. They had been running around the house trying to find a safe place. The beds were floating. The glass was flying. The roof was gone. The steep common rafters were twisting, only the joists were still intact.

The comfort room was full of black, swirling water, a combination of the flood and the dirt of the city. The bathroom door was spewing water from its cracks, spilling out over the top and squirting across the room. Kuya Boy unlocked the door and the water was up to Regie's neck.

Kuya Boy moaned and cried. "We are all going to die," he said.

"I am not going to die," said Regie. "I know how to swim."

He waded across the room and grabbed some shelves and waded back with the shelves so he could build a step and push everyone to the rafters. He pushed them up one by one. Ate Malyn was the last one to go. She was short and plump and her gown had come off and she just wore shorts and a top. Regie got her up on the top shelf and grabbed her and began to push. Her shorts split and her fat bottom popped out. She cried out and went limp. Regie wrestled her, like wrestling a slab of lechon.

"Come on! Come on!" Kuya Boy screamed at his wife.

She did not move. She did not want to be seen.

"I will just die here," she said.

"Holy Shit, get up here. You are putting his life in danger," said Kuya Boy.

Regie just kept pushing, hoisting her up to Kuya Boy. He was blind to the fat bottom. He just wanted her up there so he could get up too. The water was filthy and smelled. The wind was coming from everywhere. The ocean was spilling into the house, like the house was a cistern in the ground. From all sides the ocean came, turning the rooms into whirlpools of sewage.

Regie swam across the room to the window and climbed the grill to the rafters. He crouched there, seven meters from the family. His thoughts were on Wendell. He looked out trying to see him in the typhoon. The water was slowly receding.

"We are saved!" Regie yelled to Kuya Boy, and then he saw the last surge coming. It came out of the Coca Cola plant, a thick bubbling mass, pushing a fleet of spinning Coca Cola cars towards them.

"*Kaput, kaput* (Hang on, hang on). *Kamo Kuya Boy, kay mga awto makadi iyo balay!* (look out Kuya Boy, the cars are heading to your house!)" he shouted.

The house shuddered and the surge swirled about their bodies, as they clung to the red iron rafters. The fleet of eight red Coke cars—no longer bright—but black with mud, charged across the round-a-bout like cavalry and spilled about the house. Two hit the house, but only two, the others fell in the charge, upended and broken. The house will collapse, thought Regie. But it didn't collapse. The rooms already half full took the brunt of the surge and the water passed by.

"Regie, Regie." Kuya Boy was screaming and then as if a choir everyone was screaming. "There is a snake. There is a snake. Regie, Regie!"

Regie looked over and saw a small black snake swimming below Kuya Boy. It took him awhile to understand the family's screams, their terror. It baffled him. The snake twisted and curled in the water. He looked away ignoring the family. He had saved them. He had saved himself. He wasn't going to risk his life again because someone was afraid of a harmless black water snake.

Regie, the family, and Bobby stayed on the red bar joists for three hours until the water retreated. Ate Mely kept up an insistent cry about her belongings, everything lost. On and on she wailed and finally Kuya Boy told her to stop crying. "God has given us a second chance to live again. We all called on God, saying God, God, stop this Typhoon. That is enough."

Ate Mely worried about her belongings. Kuya Boy was glad to be alive. Regie's mind was everywhere. He was thinking about living. He was thinking that he saved a family that was not his own. He could not get the force of the wind and water out of his mind. He felt a great loss for Wendell. He worried about his family, his children in the mountains. From his view every coconut tree had fallen or broken off. The roundabout was a barren field. He could only presume that his home had been likewise damaged. Had his family been crushed? Were they alive?

A signal two typhoon is what they call it. It was the windiest and wettest night we have experienced since our arrival. Our windows are partially broken above our bed and the metal grates don't latch. The bit of glass left was like a sail on a broken spar, banging and flapping in its rail.

The early morning brought the worst. Loose tin hammering, tarps flailing wildly like terrified horses pulling against their tethers, a bell clamoring incessantly, a thin spray of water in the room and on the mosquito net, but for the most part I slept.

—From an aid worker's journal, 2014, Tacloban, Philippines

CHAPTER 3

The Roaring and The Waves

DANA LABITA

At 1:00 am Dana changed the diaper of her elderly patient. The winds had changed. They sounded like a big exhaust fan in the old wooden upstairs of the house. The lower level was concrete with solid doors and windows, but upstairs—the house built just after the war—was constructed of rough sawn mahogany, with lap siding and capiz shell windows. The floor was planked and solid, but there were cracks.

Dana's job was clear to her. She was a nurse. She checked on her comatose patient, tucked her in and made her as comfortable as possible. She swept a hair off the old woman's forehead and rested her hand on the wrinkled skin for a moment to reassure her. The other nurse and sisters were sleeping. At 1:15 am she too lay down to rest.

At 4:00 am Friday morning, Jean, the other nurse, came into her room. The house was moving.

"I am worried," Jean said. "I want to go I want to go home to my own family."

"Look at me," Dana said. "Look into my eyes. Pray. Pray for everything and accept what happens." She held Jean, squeezing comfort into her with her arms and then to comfort herself she called

Allan. No one answered. Dana tried over and over and finally got hold of Tina, her sister-in-law.

"Allan is at the house trying to get *Nanay* to stop praying," Tina said. *Nanay* was Allan's mother.

"Okay, have him call me."

For Dana her mother-in-law's faith was idolatry. Her worship was sedentary; she had to have her saints and her chair. She was a Catholic, they were all Catholic, but not like that. And then Dana prayed herself. She prayed for her family and to accept God's will and in that praying she was a nurse again—worry and motherhood swept aside by duty.

By 5:00 am the wind had magnified. Dana felt like her eardrums would burst. The sound of the air that Dana had heard earlier that morning was multiplied ten times. The house was shaking. The capiz windows were ratcheting in their frames. Emotionally she was back in Saudi Arabia, back in the emergency room, functioning as the professional she was trained to be. She did not feel nervous. She was not worried about her family. She had this feeling of control, of being able to do what needed to be done. She was concerned the patient would be covered with glass, so she and Jean tucked a sheet around her. The patient was comatose, but Dana did not see her that way.

"I am here for you." She whispered in Mommu's ear. "I will not leave you."

She felt Mommu trembling.

Jean was tense.

"Relax Jean, so this old mother will relax. Remember what I said, pray."

Jean relaxed for the moment.

Dr. Lay and Mom Edin were not with the nurses and Dana went to find them. She was worried they had gone downstairs. She did not want to leave the patient, but they also could not leave the other two sisters alone. In the house the glass in the windows and above the doors began to burst. They were spewing out of their frames and being hurled against the walls. The wind was whirling and forceful, pushing through the cracks of the house. Eighty-two-year-old Dr. Lay was trying to tie the windows shut in the bedroom of the second floor. She called to Dana and Dana went over to help. She locked the windows and knotted the strings, but above her the glass began to shatter and burst, section after section, with hammers of noise. She pulled Dr. Lay away.

Jean was calling, so Dana ran back to the patient. Jean was screaming at her, but she could barely hear. The window behind the patient was shaking. The two of them moved the bed, pulling it away from the window.

Jean was crying and telling Dana not to leave, but she left anyway to find the other two women. Dana yelled at her to "Focus, pray, don't panic, I have to get the other sisters."

The two sisters had gone downstairs. Dana was shouting at them, but they could not hear. The wind was so loud. It was pitch black. The rain that was coming in from the broken windows felt like it was cutting her hand. It was marble heavy and needle sharp.

When Dana went downstairs to find the other two women, Dr. Lay and her sister, she saw water rushing around, like a mad animal on the floor. Dr. Lay was across the room at the front door, pushing on it. She called to Dana for help. The two of them pushed together and what they thought was the wind was pushing back, and then the water was spurting over the top of the door and it collapsed, snapping, twisting, bouncing off Dana's shoulder. Dr. Lay was catapulted across the room under the piano, semi-conscious. Dana pulled her up. Her head was flopping, but she snapped awake. The water was up to their necks.

"My laptops, we must get my laptops." The doctor was crying.

"No," said Dana, and she pushed her, with her elbows, body and even her foot to the stairs. The other sister was crying in a corner of the room, just her head showing. Dana stepped from the stairs to the piano and grabbed her, pulling her to the stairs as well. The water was like a snake, twisting and writhing, and like a snake it followed them up the stairs.

Dr. Lay was calm, but blank. The house trembled. The water was waist high on the second floor. Dana did not think about her family. Her only thought was I must save these people.

The patient's bed was floating with the old woman still lying on it. Dr. Lay said. "Dana you go. I will just stay here with my sisters. You go out, but I will stay."

"No!" Dana said. Up, up! She was forceful and did not talk to Dr. Lay, like an employee, but as a patient. "You stand on this chair by the window." Dana pushed her to the chair.

In the middle of the mud and the gnashing of the wind, four of them stood, praying, crying, terrified, except for the patient on her mattress, who floated comatose.

Dana repeated parts of the Rosary, the ten Holy Mary's, and said, "Lord if this is the last moment of my life that is okay, but please save my family. I accept your will."

Jean, the other nurse was looking toward the window and saw a plastic barrel floating toward them. She called to Dana.

"This is a savings device," Dana said.

"Do you know how to swim?" Jean asked.

"No."

"Just go like this," and she paddled with her hands.

"We will not go without the patients. No, we cannot go. It is too cold and they are too old." And to the sisters, she said. "We will not leave you."

"Thank you," said the doctor.

When the drum got to the window of the house, a rat jumped out of it and grabbed Dana by the leg. It held on her skin like a terrified child, clinging and shaking. The drum had a rope in it and Dana grabbed the rope and tied it to herself and the sisters. The house was shaking and getting ready to collapse. Dana does not remember how long they stood there tied together and tethered with a piece of rope to a plastic barrel. It seemed like seconds.

Dana looked out the broken window and was not sure what she was seeing. She saw a pregnant woman holding a wire, with the wind pushing her back and forth, like she was floating, holding an umbrella.

An old man was hanging on some power lines. The roof of a house was whirling around, slow and ponderously like a big wheel and children were floating like rubber dolls. She stood and watched, her mind faded and vacant, like a shell on the shore. "I am not sure," she whispered. "I am not sure...."

At three this morning, one of the Canadians knocked on our bedroom door. I didn't hear anything. I was sleeping soundly. Deb did.

"Someone's knocking."

It took a while for the words to reach a conscious part of my mind. Eventually they did and then the conscious took over and the sleep disappeared.

"Yes," I said, "What is it?"

"There is a leak," she said.

"A leak?"

"Yes a leak."

This is Tacloban. There is no house in Tacloban with a secure and complete roof, at least not that I have seen. Leaks happen. They are part of life. A drip from the roof is not something to wake people over. It is not something to knock on a bedroom door at three in the morning to discuss.

I lay there with Deb thinking about the leak, wondering if it was a leak that was getting the tent people in the living room wet, or just the back bathroom floor or the back slop sink. Sleep seemed better, but the leak was a pressing item now that it had been knocked into my door and into my mind.

I got up finally, expecting to see the Canadian girl waiting, but she had done her thing, awoken me, and crawled back to her tent and the comfort of her sleeping bag.

I peered around at the floor in the Living room, where the tents were and she slept. It looked dry. I looked at the kitchen. It too was dry. I opened the door to the back hallway, where the slop sink and back bathroom were, where last night the floor was wet from leaks. The floor was still wet, but not much wetter.

I went back to bed and lay there thinking about leaks, trying to sleep. Tossing and turning.

—From an aid worker's journal, 2014, Tacloban, Philippines

CHAPTER 4

A Sea of Sand

SAMUEL MAGDUA

P art of Samuel's initial grief was his grief in God. He grieved for his community, but he also grieved for his miracle. He did not understand or even believe in miracles, yet he had become one and felt he was undeserving. He grieved because God had spared he and his family and there was seemingly no reason for his being spared. He found God had become personal. He did not understand a personal God and it was frightening to have a God he did not understand, one who would destroy what was beautiful and safe and save someone who drank *tuba* and gambled at cockfights. God had come too close and become too real and too unpredictable. It haunted him.

One month after Yolanda Samuel attempted fishing. He bought a boat for twelve thousand pesos. He cast off near Ramil's home, paddling slowly. There was wind and some waves. A few firemen were hauling a body eaten by crabs from the shallows. They had a chainsaw and were cutting the brush and salvaging the dead. He looked away, but he had seen enough. He vomited over the side and cried. He called to the powerful One, but he heard nothing. He felt vulnerable. The ocean frightened him. Terrified, he paddled to shore.

"I don't know what is wrong with me," he said. "I hear the word Yolanda and I cry. I see my neighbors, the ones that are gone and even the ones that are here and I cry. I look at my house and I cry. Maybe I am not a tough guy anymore."

Samuel, Geraldine and Sheila Mae moved to Samar, Geraldine's family home, the home she had been running to for twenty-six years. They stayed there for six weeks, away from the sea, away from the destroyed homes and dead neighbors, but not away from Yolanda. In the morning Samuel would walk the forests of Samar, destroyed as they were by the typhoon, the sound of chainsaws ripping the mountain calm. Samar had been forested by coconut palms before the storm. They were massive forests, planted to supply the coconut oil factories. Yolanda had snapped and uprooted these manmade forests, harvesting the mountains, reaping and letting lie fallow the earth, exposing its once shaded ground to the sun. It was ugly destruction. He walked hour after hour. He tried to reason out his life, his survival, and how to begin again.

It took him four months, but Samuel Magdua started fishing again. It was hard. In two hours Yolanda had ripped away half a century of toughness exposing an underbelly of vulnerability, exposing fears he did not know he had and did not want to know he had.

Samuel struggles each moment to understand God. Oddly it isn't the destruction and power he doesn't understand. Samuel has experienced God's power and destruction. It is his deliverance and the deliverance of his family that he cannot understand. During the storm the roof had floated on the walls of the house and it had stayed. It shouldn't have stayed. The family held on, each child and every woman. They couldn't have held on. Every one of them was sprayed with shrapnel and no one died or was injured. His only explanation was that he had experienced the miraculous.

Samuel's God did not do impossible things for people such as him. This is what worries him and frightens him. It keeps him from fishing the Amihan's where the huge rollers challenge every fiber of a fisherman's boat and body. If, and he is trying to answer the if, if God saved him… then why? Why him?

Samuel—a year later

For some who were not there, Typhoon Yolanda is a horrible memory, a storm for the history books. For Samuel, the day the Kabungan wind rode again, sweeping from its hiding place to show its power, is a day he lives in, each waking moment.

He remembers his oldest sister Alice who was washed away and never found.

He can see the boy with the bubbles more clearly now than during the storm. The boy haunts him. "I could have saved him. I am not afraid of the dead, like the others. I told them, but they could not do it. They could not touch him."

He remembers those that were wholesaled; The Pieto family of seven members, the Antolan family of thirteen, the Enunciabo family of five, the Roxas family of seven, and others—faces that tumble over him and suffocate him.

He remembers the three waves that came over the peninsula and hit them. They are like a nightmare he lives in and works in, water, a wave, a wasteland.

In December, when Typhoon Ruby—the strongest storm of 2014—hit Tacloban he sought safety for his family in the evacuation center. "Geraldine has a phobia about typhoons. I immediately encouraged our family to transfer."

There is a peace in their family that was not there before. The monthly fights over money and gambling are over.

"I do not run away to Samar anymore," says Geraldine. "I am staying here now and caring for Sheila Mae. I am wondering how to make our future better. I am wondering how to build our house." The house itself is ramshackle. Samuel's home is on Romualdez land, no build land. Rebuilding is a political process rather than a humanitarian one. Samuel knows it has been left untouched by aid or reconstruction because the plan is to recapture it for individual use. The refuse of the storm still litters everything around them. The externals that were destroyed in Yolanda are still destroyed. The lives surrounding them are survivor's lives in different places of recovery. His brother Henry drinks, sings and plays his guitar next door.

Samuel says, "I will let myself cry if I need to cry. God's will be that I would survive. If there were no God I would not be here. He has so many plans for me. The Lord God has so many things for me to do."

Samuel is fishing as he has always fished, facing the dangers of the sea, not running. He wades out to his boat, moored ten meters from shore as the sun sets over Cancabato Bay, he lets his engine run and secures his nets and slowly motors out to sea, past the Daniel Z. Romualdez Airport, into the Leyte Gulf, alone except for his God, in the darkness of the night.

I saw a boy hit by a motorcycle. The older brother of one of the notorious escapees had led me to his brother, convict number eleven, on the Airport wall. The older brother was nervous for his "at large" brother and after connecting his brother and me he left hurriedly. We followed. A boy leaped out and the older brother hit him with the motorcycle. There was a tangle of legs, a rolling of the body, like when a dog is hit, spinning around in the road with tumbling and waving legs. The boy's sandal went flying and the cars from the other direction ran over it, and then a truck ran over it. The boy got up and slapped his right leg by the knee. He kept limping and slapping his leg keeping one eye on his sandal getting run over by vehicles. Then the boy retrieved his sandal and walked off slapping his right leg by the knee. The older brother who had stopped, but was worried at the gathering crowd, was happy to leave.

—From an aid worker's journal, 2014, Tacloban, Philippines

C H A P T E R   4

A Sea of Sand

NOEL LITO

ate in the afternoon on Friday the water receded to just over a foot. Noel and the survivors gathered at the guard's bidding. Throughout the city jail on all of the levels convicts pried themselves from the walls and floors, as if they had been plastered there. Noel stood wet and brown in the courtyard, the water to his knees. Some of his cellmates had lost clothes and stood in underwear or wrapped in muddy unfitting garments. The guards did a head count. No one had died. Twenty-four of the BCD's (Batang City Jail) had escaped out the exhaust vents and the open ceiling. The guards recorded the information. They did not attempt to form a search party for the escapees. There was a dullness about everyone. It was 4:00 pm. Hours had elapsed, but the hours seemed like moments and they seemed like years.

The city jail, like every other structure in the city was full of black sticky mud and debris. The prisoners were tasked to clean up the prison. Noel worked alongside his fellow inmates. He carried mud in his hands, scraping it from the cells and dumping it in a growing pile. There was a light rain that fell intermittently. At 6:00 pm the kitchen boy cooked rice and Noel ate rice and four ounces of sardines for his first meal of the day. He drank rainwater that had collected.

It was black when the evening head count was complete. There was no power and no backup power. Everything had been flooded and destroyed. Noel slept on bare wood Friday night, but he slept and there was shelter and food.

The prisoners had personal stashes of food in the rafters of the prison. When family and visitors came they always brought rice and the inmates would store it and use it to supplement their normal diet of bread and whatever else they were given. Saturday morning Noel and his fellow convicts began to clean up, starting where they had left off the night before. They had no bread, no coffee, but they had these stashes of rice and a can of sardines. A few relations of the prisoners stopped by and requested rice. The inmates gave out their personal stash to relatives and visitors, but before the day was out they were sharing rice with the jail officers and guards, who were requesting it for their families. Everyone who knew that they had stocks of food came and by Saturday afternoon the stocks were gone.

Noel cleaned all day Saturday. There were no tools and everything was done by hand. The water had left a black sludge that coated everything like ink. He ate a small bowl of rice and one-half a can of sardines for lunch. There was nothing to do but work and wonder what the situation was outside. He worked like this, knowing he had no food for dinner.

It was not until Sunday that Noel and the other prisoners began to understand the scope of the devastation in San Jose and surrounding areas. The survivors from outside looking for food and checking on family members came bringing story after horrible story of death and destruction. Some of the guards left to check on their families. The new shift of guards did not come.

The inmates began to pray for a miracle for their families. Noel's wife Maricris and her family lived near the astrodome in Magallanes, a washed out area. There was no food or water in the prison Sunday and Sunday morning the men were kept locked in their cells. In Noel's cell forty-three men crowded, hungry and dirty black. They milled about their cells all day,

"Food." Someone shouted and the shout was picked up until the prison was filled with the chant of "food, food, food."

There was a raw power of unanimity than ran through the walls—that of jailed men desperate to be freed, needing to help their families, but helpless to do so. The prison was a bomb waiting to explode. The men shouted at the guards, cursed the prison and shook the bars on their cells. The day turned into night. Noel shrank into his bunk and huddled there hungry and scared.

Monday morning was grey, wet and humid. There was still no food or water. At 11:00 am an assembly was called and all the inmates were gathered in the courtyard. They were told they could leave for forty-eight hours to check on their families. This was a compromise by the prison, but it had no choice. The jail was surrounded by death, hunger, and destroyed people.

Noel had been in the city jail five years and three months. He shuffled out the doors, like all the other men. He was fearful for his family, desperate to find them. He was hungry and thirsty. He was scarred and violated by men on both sides of the law and by his own actions. In some ways he was still a child, in some ways an old man. At the age of twenty–two, forty–eight hours of freedom was not going to be enough.

Two months later Noel is number eleven on Tacloban's most wanted list.

He spends his day with his wife in their shack in Magallanes near the Astrodome. In the weeks and months after Yolanda the survivors have salvaged the wreckage of a city and built makeshift shelters. Magallanes is crowded with these shelters and people in them.

Noel is doing some cooking, some cleaning and laundry around the house, trying to make himself useful and life easier for his wife. Occasionally his brother gives him some odd jobs. All the neighbors know he is at large, but most of the neighbors are relatives. He ran into one of the city guards, who told him he should report back to the jail.

The government has put a shoot-to-kill order out on Noel. All of the escaped men—listed on the airport wall—are considered dangerous. There is no distinction between those like Noel trapped in a system, and the rapists and murderers he was incarcerated with. There is always the possibility some overzealous policeman will take the "shoot-to-kill" order seriously. Anger is escalating. The police, like their neighbors, are under severe emotional and physical stress. It is in the air blowing like the smells, from place to place and often lying thick and stagnant, like gas in the bilge of a boat, waiting to blow. So Noel stays in the house most of the time. He is very careful to do no wrong.

When his pregnant wife delivers he plans to go somewhere else, perhaps Manila where he can disappear. But for now, waiting for Maricris to deliver their first child, he does not feel he can leave, so he hides in plain sight, known to all who truly want to know, and goes about his days, very like his days in prison, quietly and peacefully, trying to be useful, trying not to disturb.

Maricris is always wary. "Do not go out now Noel," she whispers from their door. "There is someone I don't know."

"Is it clear? I need to use the toilet?" Noel asks. He always asks.

"You have to wait," she replies. And he waits.

"Okay, you can go, but cover your tattoos."

When he goes, she follows him and stands by the community toilet, until it is safe for him to return.

"Come here," he says in their makeshift home. "You make me safe." He touches her, and she responds.

Noel—a year later

Slowly Noel is integrating into Tacloban life. Unlike others, Yolanda has given him his freedom. He is making the most of it. His son Wilmar is almost a year old. Noel is working as a contract painter for a company. His wife Maricris gets up early, makes him breakfast and packs his lunch. She is doing her job. He is doing his. She is a good friend. They are happy. He is worrying less about the authorities.

He confesses hopefully that the authorities are not interested in him, or that his case files have been washed away, or the complainants have left Tacloban.

But he is careful to be low key. He wears glasses and a hat when venturing out. If he sees a policeman he will filter into the crowd or change direction and walk a side street. He does not cause trouble in the community. He and Maricris attend the Redemptorist Church Sunday at 5:00 pm. They never miss the afternoon service.

He is still a member of the BSL's (Batang Samar Leyte Gang). Every three months there is a quarterly meeting to inform every member of the gang, inside and out, of the donations, expenditures and who the officers are.

There is dirty work to be done on occasion. The gang leaders meet and discuss the gang's business. If action is needed they take it.

The Head—known as the Mayor—of the BSL's has been in touch with him. On one occasion, six months after his freedom, a man slipped a note under his door with a phone number on it for Noel to call.

It was the Mayor's number. "Hello my friend," the Mayor said, when Noel called.

"Hello Mayor," replied Noel.

"There is a man in your community, a bad man, who has a problem with me," said the Mayor. "I may need your help. You know where he lives and when he comes and goes."

"Mayor, I have a family now. I have a new baby. Please may I be excused?"

There was silence on the phone and then the Mayor said, "*Okay lang*, it is fine. I understand. I will find another one."

John Paul, the "bad man," was killed a few days later by some hit men. Noel did not warn John Paul, though he could have. "I would be dead by sunset, if I did," he says. "It is the way it is. I am more afraid of the Mayor than the police. The Mayor can eliminate police too."

Noel is tattooed with a number 22 on his left buttock, the number of the BSL's, a number consecrated with blood in the Muntinlupa National Bilibid Prison years ago. There was a gang war and 500 members of the BSL's were involved. Only 22 survived. All the BSL's are tattooed with number 22. And Noel's number—hidden from view—is known by those who need to know. He is a member for life unless he erases the tattoo. If so he will answer for that and it will not be a friendly answer.

"Maybe you should leave the gang," Maricris said to him after John Paul had been killed.

"How can I do that?" he asked. "If I go back to jail I will be as good as dead. If I remove my tattoo they will beat me."

"How badly?"

"I don't know, maybe break some bones, I don't know."

"What should we do?"

"Nothing, it will be okay. I need the gang."

Noel was tested again a few months later. The Mayor asked him to do some dirty jobs, or give 20,000 pesos.

"What do they want you to do?" Maricris asked him.

"Nothing, it's okay, the Mayor said I don't have to pay this time and he let me off. It's okay."

"What about tomorrow?"

"Tomorrow, will be okay."

How then must I respond to this conflict of goals? The goal to push for heaven on earth, for there the horizons of heaven stretch before each person with equality and ownership is only an unimaginable farce. There all the earthly tables of power and intelligence will have been overturned, flipped violently over like Jesus flung over the table in the temple two thousand years ago. Heaven, as CS Lewis described it in The Great Divorce, where opportunity stretches forth eternally, in direct divergence to the poverty-stricken communities that are constructed here. How do I as a Christian speak out or act out God's plan for man of fairness, justice and eternal hope?

—From an aid worker's journal, 2014, Tacloban, Philippines

CHAPTER 4

A Sea of Sand

ALLAN LABITA

One of the bodies the water carried toward the ocean was baby Coleen. It carried her down Allan's narrow alley, across the Daniel Z. Romualdez Highway, past the downed Rima tree that had stood for four hundred years, into the mangrove forest, which was now a jungle of roots and branches. A web of mango branches had caught her and held her like a fly on a web and she lay there high and dry until a neighbor saw her and yelled. Allan and Arman came stumbling and crying to her. She was still alive, but barely. They tried CPR, but she needed oxygen.

Allan wrapped her in a shirt from the yellow house and started to run to the hospital. It was three kilometers to the hospital over piles of what had been homes, trees, cars and ocean bottom. He saw a young athletic friend by the name of Bikoy standing by and he knew Bikoy could do it. He knew he couldn't.

"Take her to the hospital. Go," he said.

Three of the family and Bikoy carrying Coleen ran to the hospital. He watched them briefly. Bikoy ran in ragged clothes, black and dirty from the storm, cradling Coleen softly in his arms, while his legs churned and pumped, running, climbing, rushing, hopeful and afraid. The other three were trailing, trying to keep up, but not able.

It was 11:00 am Friday when Bikoy left with baby Coleen. Allan looked for Ax and his mother. He pulled out six dead people from two different houses, but he left them on the street. He wandered up and down his street. If he saw a dead person he pulled him or her out to make sure it wasn't his mother or Ax. He saw four dead children in the mango grove, where Coleen had lain. He saw dead on the rooftops, dead hanging from wires, dead on the terraces of destroyed homes.

At 1:00 pm a neighbor started yelling. Allan, Tiyo Andong is over here, over here!" Tiyo Andong was Uncle Alex and Allan rushed to where he was, thinking Ax would be with him.

Uncle Alex was lying in some rubble. He was okay. "Did you find Ax?" were his first words.

"Not yet."

"You find him."

"I will."

"How are you, there is blood in your shorts."

"Not so good."

"Would you like water?"

"Yes."

"Coke?" There was Coke here and there from the *sari-sari* stores that were destroyed.

"Okay."

"Cigarette?"

"Yes."

"You are bleeding, where is that coming from?"

Allan pulled up Uncle Alex's shorts and he had a deep wound in his thigh that splayed open and shivered in the light.

Allan carried him to the yellow house. The rest of the family was sitting and in shock. Aileen was lying on the table dead. The children were quiet. Allan was the only one moving around.

"Stay with my kids," he said looking at them. "Give them water."

"We have no water!"

Allan cut the plastic utility line that fed the house. "There," he said. "There is water."

"Where are you going?" asked Uncle Alex.

"I am going to find mother and Ax."

Someone called to him about some bodies in the debris. He saw curly hair like his mother in a pile. It was not his mother. He dragged the body to the street. Everyone was taking bodies to the street.

He spent the day searching. His neighbors were not much help. He greeted them. They looked at him like zombies, blank and unknowing. It was exhausting work. The debris was mountainous and thick with heavy sludge. It was unending. At some point the blackness of Yolanda gave way to light, but he did not notice and then dusk came and the dusk surprised him. He made his way back to the yellow house. Everyone was there. It had begun to rain. There was no roof. Everyone was crying. There was no food. He looked at his children and was worried. He needed to find food. He needed a plan. He needed to find Ax.

After the storm many in Allan's neighborhood transferred to the home of the counselor located on the same street as Allan's house. It was an expansive three-story mansion and lightly damaged. The large steel doors had broken out of the wall and so the counselor's compound was exposed to all the "commoners," and in an uncommon act of generosity, the counselor allowed neighbors to shelter there Friday evening. If he had done this before the storm, many would have lived who died. Allan's family settled in the living room of the counselor's house with other survivors. Allan helped everybody transfer, got them settled and walked back outside to the main road. There he met an exodus of people coming from the barangays north and east of him. North of him was Barangay 88, east of him was Barangay 85 and 86 and the airport. Allan watched this exodus, trying to take it in and understand the scope of the damage.

He saw a familiar face on the road. It was Dana, his wife. She was wet and dirty and her hair was matted to her skull except where it was tangled. He recognized her among the thousands who were walking by. She did not recognize Allan. He was wearing a very wet sweatshirt, striped shorts, sandals and no dentures.

Allan rushed up to her. "Dana!"

She did not answer. "Dana! This is Allan." He shook her.

Dana heard but did not hear. She felt like she was in a fog. She had walked from her night shift, but it wasn't morning. It was late afternoon, dusk. She was traumatized. She had heard on the road home that Ax was missing.

"Lucky for us, Phill, Yugi and Princess are alive. Mother is dead. Aileen is dead. Coleen is dead. Uncle is hurt."

Dana had mixed emotions. She wanted to say things, cry and shout out where was Ax? What did you do with Ax? But at first nothing would come out.

"Where are they? Where is Ax? Is he safe?" she cried.

Allan hugged her and Dana collapsed. He carried her to the counselor's house. "Oh my god, oh my god, oh my god Yolanda." He felt light and sick. He felt the dark gloom of failure envelope him as he carried his wife. Her weight was now his weight and it was more weight than he could bear. He wanted to be cast away, crucified. He wanted Ax. He wanted everything they did together to happen again. He wanted to wrestle, jump, play and fly kites with him again.

Allan settled Dana in the counselor's house. Eventually she got up and began to shout, but not at Allan. She shouted at God. "You did not save our family. You gave me strength to be strong and you take away my family? I do not trust you anymore. Why did you do this to my family?" And later she shouted at God again. "You have promised to keep my family safe. What have I done?"

It was a long night. The counselor's family offered everyone a few hotdogs. It rained and thundered, things that are common after a storm, yet nothing was common to the survivors. They heard in every sound Yolanda's warning of what had been and will come again.

Allan told Dana that he saved ten people next door. It meant nothing to her. Jo, the godfather of Ax, was at the counselor's house with them. Slowly the night quieted down and the sorrow rested. Only

Dana and Godfather Jo were up.

"Do you know?" said Dana. "Ax is still alive. He is being cared for under a tree."

"Okay, okay," he said. "You can sleep now."

6:00 am Saturday morning, day two, the wind woke them up. The broken roofs and drying refuse rustled and chattered. It was windy, but the sky was blue and the sun shone. Some of the neighbors heard the counselor's wife telling the counselor to, "Get all these people out of my house, because they will make it dirty and you will have to feed them." Of course the survivors heard her shouting; they were meant to hear. The word spread and everyone left. Allan and his family moved onto the street. The stench of death was in the air.

Slowly Dana, who had spent the night crying and in hysterics, began to respond to the circumstances. The family moved back into the yellow house. The first sight that greeted Dana was Aileen, still lying on the table. There was fresh blood on Aileen's neck and in her ear, but Dana was more concerned with Uncle Alex, who was drooling and slurring his speech. He had suffered a stroke in the night. Baby Coleen was at the St. Peter's Hospital. She had died for lack of oxygen.

At 7:00 am Saturday morning Allan made a sling from some sticks and a sheet. He enlisted five men to take Uncle Alex to St. Peter's. The debris made walking impassable, so one of the men cleared a path ahead of the four. Tiya Nene, Uncle Alex's wife followed them.

At 8:00 am Allan went out to find food. He went to the warehouse of Johnson and Johnson, thinking he could salvage rice and canned goods. The roof had collapsed and it was dangerous to go in, but there were cases of sanitary napkins scattered about. Allan grabbed all he could carry. Many of the women, including Dana, Tina, Armida and three immediate neighbors were dealing with abnormal menstruation, so the napkins were needed.

At 2:00 pm Tiya Nene returned to the yellow house. Uncle Alex had died in the hospital.

At 4:00 pm Allan's mother was found. Allan carried her corpse to the yellow house.

By 6:00 pm Saturday the blackness of the city had enveloped them. The usual sounds were gone. No dog barked. No rooster crowed. No bird sang. No two-cycle engines spit and sputtered. No trucks roared. There was no muted laughter or drinking voices of the night. The light was gone, and to stave off the blackness Allan built a bonfire from some of the debris. He saw other fires here and there in the distance. Between the fires was only fear.

Sunday, the third day after the storm, began as Saturday had ended. The reality of their situation began to settle in. Everything they had prepared for in the case of an emergency was gone. Sunday morning Dana and Allan walked to the Robinson's store, four kilometers away, that was being looted. Allan took five packs of hotdogs, but he gave one pack to a woman who was also trying to loot, but whom the crowds squeezed out—she needed food for her children. He stole some diapers, two cartons of sanitary napkins, betadine, alcohol and bread. He took a toy.

Sunday afternoon Allan, Tina, Arnel and Arman carried the bodies of their mother, Aileen, Uncle Alex and baby Coleen to the St. Peter's funeral home, three kilometers away. They left the bodies on the lawn with fifty-seven other bodies. They returned exhausted as night fell.

Monday, the fourth day, was more of the same, but the immediate need was medicine. Everybody was looking for medicine, everybody was bleeding. There was frantic need for tetanus vaccine. Allan and Dana went to the Mayor's office.

Allan talked to an official there and requested medicine for the community.

The official said, "They can come here. Send the people here."

"No they can't," Allan answered.

"Why?"

"It is too far. They would die. Just help us, my wife can give the injections."

"Really, okay," and he gave them eighty-eight shots of tetanus which Dana administered in the neighborhood.

At a local drug store that was being looted, Dana was able to retrieve some insulin, anti-hypertension meds, anti-diarrhea and other drugs.

The days seemed endless, the nights oppressive. Dana began to shut down. She wasn't sleeping. The children were not getting proper food. They were losing weight and energy. Allan was tasked with taking care of the dead and finding food for the family. His brother Kim was unresponsive, still in shock. What Allan wanted to do was find Ax. Ax was always on his mind. He never walked anywhere without looking, asking people if they had seen a seven-year-old boy, wearing a number eight Kobe Bryant jersey, a yellow one. No one had.

On Tuesday, the fifth day after the storm, Allan's brother-in-law showed up from Biliran, one hundred and ten kilometers away. He was driving a motorcycle.

Allan sent him home. "Go," he said. "Go now, leave. Get a truck for my family."

"What happened?"

"It doesn't matter, you go, as fast as you can, go."

So Allan's brother-in-law left. He sped off on his motorcycle, propelled by the image of Allan shouting and urging him on. He remembered Allan later, a crippled apparition of a street walker, with black hair standing like horns, his mouth open, his teeth gone, his eyes wide, yelling, "Go, go, go!"

Kim, Arnel, Tina and Allan went Sunday night to retrieve the bodies of their dead family from St. Peter's. In the morning the corpses were being buried in one of the many mass graves. One of the great travesties of this storm was the loss of the "sacred burial tradition" unavailable to relatives. It is part of Filipino society to consecrate their dead and the burial ritual is a large part of the preparation. Allan and hundreds of other survivors went to incredible lengths to provide the tribute their culture mandates.

At St. Peter's, Allan's three siblings refused to traverse the horror before them. Allan did. He stuffed cloth in his nose. He vomited on the ground. He walked through the lifeless and one by one he dragged his dead family to his living family. He stepped over corpses that gaped at him with open lips and bugged eyes. One man's arm was stuck in the air, his hand plaintively crying to be taken too. "From now on no horror movie will frighten me." Allan says. "Drowning is so horrible. The people are bloated. Eyes are coming out of the faces. Some eyes have fallen out. There are holes in their flesh."

The four of them carried their dead family six kilometers to Memorial Gardens.

On Thursday, the sixth day, Allan buried the dead they had carried to Memorial Gardens. He placed Uncle Alex, Aileen, Mother and baby Coleen in three concrete bunkers. Baby Coleen he tucked into the arms of her mother Aileen. He cemented the bunkers shut with cement they had salvaged from a construction site.

At 10:00 pm the truck from Biliran arrived and at 11:00 pm everyone was loaded and on their way to Biliran. All except Allan who had stayed to find Ax. The family had become a distraction. Food and shelter were not important. Finding Ax was.

His first night alone was terrifying. Allan went to the second floor of the yellow house and sat there for a long time thinking about where and how to start.

He talked to God. "I did not want them to leave," he said in the loneliness of the night. "I wanted someone to stay with me. They are weak. So am I. God, give me the strength. I will face anything."

On the seventh day he set out walking, two hours in one direction, and then two hours in another. He looked for dead. Someone would say, "There are a lot of dead over there." And so that is where he would go.

"Have you seen dead people?"

"Have you seen a boy wearing a yellow jersey?"

"Have you seen any dead children?"

"Yeah there are dead over there," someone often said.

Allan would go there. "Oh, my god, oh God, where is he? Where is Ax?"

The second night alone Allan prepared the yellow house. He put a pipe in one place, a machete in another and a piece of re-rod in another. He had a sword he had found that he had kept by his side. He put weapons where he could grab them. Looters were getting desperate. He built a bonfire to bring him some comfort. He didn't dare venture out after 6:00 pm or he would get lost. The landmarks disappeared in the night. Tacloban was no longer a living city.

On the following day, day eight, a boy called to him and said, "Allan, is your son missing?"

"Yes."

"There are five floating, and one looks like him," the boy said.

"Where, oh god, where?"

"Do you want to see them?"

"Yes I want to see him".

The bodies were floating eight feet from the shore. "Where is that boy you are telling me that looks like Ax?

"In the middle."

"Give me that bamboo." Allan fished the boy in. It was not Ax.

"Thank you, call me again," Allan said.

The horror of what he was seeing became transfixed in his mind. He saw a friend lying dead and another friend with his baby lying dead. He took time to cover the dead, as did others. He went to the Astrodome where multiple bodies lay. He stood among them, turning slowly around, wobbling like a top, looking for anybody that looked like Ax.

On day eight Lemuel, a thirty-five year old friend, came by with his family.

"Are you leaving?" Allan asked.

"We are going to Cebu. It is not safe here."

"Good luck, see you around."

Are you staying by yourself?" Lemuel asked.

"Yes."

There was an awkward silence and Lemuel left with his family. Minutes later he came running back. "I am staying with you," he told Allan. "I have decided to stay and help you find Ax."

"Thank you, thank you so much." That was the end of the conversation.

Allan would search and Lemuel would be at his side.

On day nine Bikoy—the athlete, who is twenty-four and who had carried Coleen to St. Peter's—stopped by. He was on his way to Manila with his family on a C130. They were driving in a van, but stopped to check on Allan.

"Where you going?" Allan asked.

"Manila to family," Bikoy answered.

"Good."

"And you?"

"I am staying to find Ax."

"I will stay with you."

Bikoy ran to the van. "Dad, I am staying with *Manong* (older brother)."

There were three of them now.

On the tenth day Allan needed his friends more so than before. Lack of sleep, little food and water were giving him body cramps. He was tiring, his leg, injured in the typhoon was becoming more and more crippled.

Lemuel had gotten a gun from his uncle, a lawyer. Allan had gotten a rifle from a friend in a neighboring barangay. The armory on the end of the peninsula had washed out and guns were leaching into the neighborhoods.

That night Lemuel, Bikoy and Allan heard looters knocking on a neighbor's door.

"Stay, stay," said Lemuel. "We have to listen to where the sound is coming from."

The three crept downstairs. When Lemuel shouted they ran out with their guns and knives. Allan and Lemuel both shot in the air and then chased the robbers to the San Jose Bridge. It was a planned operation, because the chased men jumped off the bridge into a waiting boat.

The three slept little.

In his mind Allan purposed to find Ax, "before we get killed here."

On the eleventh day, Lemuel and Allan saw the counselor, standing on his parapet like a Caesar, surveying his lands. His hands were on his rail; his chest was puffed out like a proud cock. He was the man who had closed his home to the survivors.

"Hah, look, he makes a good target," said Lemuel

Allan lined up his long gun in a crack. He set the sites of his rifle on the counselor's face.

"Don't shoot him," said Lemuel.

The counselor stood there oblivious. Allan caressed the trigger.

Another time Allan stood on a bridge parapet.

"What are you doing?" asked Lemuel.

"I am not going to jump. I am just thinking," answered Allan.

On the afternoon of the eleventh day Allan did not search. He stayed at the yellow house and thought about what had happened, how the wind and water had come and where it had gone. He thought about where Ax could have gone, what was possible.

On day twelve Allan woke Lemuel and Bikoy from their sleep.

"I know where he is."

"You know where he is?" questioned Bikoy.

"I am sure I know. We have to bring our jungle boyo and knife and shoes.

"Have you seen him?"

"No, but I have a feeling."

"I can't," said Lemuel. "I am sorry, but I have become afraid of the dead. I will just wait."

Ax was found buried under rubble so thick and suffocating that his body had not decomposed. It did not smell. He was lying with his head on his hands, curled up on his side, like he had always slept, in different days. He was found fifty meters from the yellow house.

It has been four months and Allan has yet to rest. Finding Ax has not lifted the darkness of the loss. Allan finds words to share how he feels, but they are inadequate. He feels the hurtful consequence of his society's greed more so than ever before. International aid has been usurped and doled out unfairly. The horrors of Yolanda have destroyed his community; it ripped off the guise of human decency in some people. In all, Yolanda exposed their frailties.

In the family home Kim sits blank and silent, as he has since Coleen suffocated at the hospital with no oxygen. Allan accepts Kim's depression and do the others, giving him unlimited time to grieve.

There are three saints of his mothers in one corner of the house. The Black Jesus, the St. Anthony, and the Immaculate Conception. Allan does not burn candles to them. But someone does.

Late in the evening, when the children are sleeping, he repairs three kites. "There is a tomorrow, Dana," he says. "The children must dream. They must play." And in the morning his angel, the kite angel, surprises them again.

Allan—one year later

Every Friday afternoon or Sunday afternoon, whichever works for the rest of the family, Allan, Dana, Phill, Yugi and Bridgette visit the tombs at Memorial Gardens. There are four new tombs and Allan's father's existing grave. The family burns candles. They place flowers. They say a few words quietly and privately to the past family members. This is a time of unity, remembrance and thankfulness for lives they were able to share, even for a short time.

What Yolanda took away, Allan will never forget. He does not want to forget, to forget will not allow him to receive what Yolanda gave. The earth grows out of sacrifice, for man the sacrifice must be received. Allan receives it.

Ax is as present in his life as he was the day he was lost to Yolanda. Allan remembers the bonfire the afternoon he found Ax, built so he could see his son one last night. Ax was wearing his Kobe Bryant jersey, the yellow one, under a grey and red sweatshirt, which was Dana's favorite, one she had brought Ax from Saudi Arabia years before.

There have been many changes. Nothing is the same. Allan is working. Dana is not. This is by her choice. She is a mother.

Allan, Dana, Phill, Yugi and Bridgette have moved to a new place. They built a modest home on inherited land. It is not far from his mother's ancestral home by the yellow house. His other siblings still live there. Tina married an architect, who works in Dubai. Franco, Aileen's husband, the merchant marine stationed in the Baltic Sea during Yolanda, visited one time. He drank heavily, trying to rinse away his grief. Allan tried to console him, but Franco was inconsolable. He is back on the ship now, back in the Baltic Sea.

The home that Dana and Allan built provides much that he did not have living with his extended family. It offers shelter and comfort, but it also gives to Allan and Dana something more.

He remembers a conversation between them a year earlier.

Phill, their oldest, was standing at the bedroom door listening.

"I wonder if the typhoon will break the house?" he asked.

"Probably," Allan replied.
"We will pray to God it doesn't," Dana said.
Mother just grunted from the lazy chair.
"If it does, we can build a better one."
"That's a dream," said Dana.

We are back in Tacloban and I slept like hell. I see now why Debbi wanted to leave so she could rest, and why Nicole, the Canadian girl, wanted to cover her ears and shut out the noises at least for a moment. The city is a dog pack. In three months the dogs have bred out of the storm and flood like insects, and at night when other sounds subside, they bark in waves across the city. Far in the distance, the howls and cries begin, and then another pack responds and joins the chorus. Slowly the cries peal across the city, rising, clashing, over and over and over again, waves of baying carry through the night. In Sogod Bay the sound never ceased as well, but it was the waves and wind. There is a difference. This is a discordant, grating sound, fractious and mournful.

—From an aid worker's journal, 2014, Tacloban, Philippines

CHAPTER 4

A Sea of Sand

DOLOR LINGO

O f the eighteen members of Dolor's family who had taken refuge in her mother's house, only five survived: Dante, Dolor, Dolor's sister Melinda, a nephew and Dante Junior. Six are missing: Dolor's mother and five nieces and nephews. Seven bodies were recovered: Auntie Jane and her one year-old grandson, Nenita, one of Nenita's sons, and Dante and Dolor's children Carl, Daniel and Princess Diana.

When the Hot Chile workers found Carl and Daniel, Dante knew they would be dead. He prayed to God to "Give me strength." There was a small crowd gathered when he reached his children under the beam, but he was the one to lift it. He cradled Phil on his left shoulder, Daniel on his right. He carried them to the sala of a neighbor's house. He spoke loudly over them, but for himself. "Lord give me strength. You are the creator. You are source of good things. I know that my sons are gone. I remember the book of Hebrews, everyone is appointed to die. I remembered the life of Job. God you are the Creator and the Judge."

Friday night and Saturday no one ate. They drank only their tears, which did not seem to end. When Princess Diana was found they laid her with the boys.

By Saturday afternoon the bodies were beginning to decompose. The odor became overwhelming.

A neighbor told Dante gently, "The children are decomposing. You have to bury them. You cannot wait for the rescue teams."

Sunday Morning, Dante, with a shovel he found in a neighbor's house dug a six-foot grave. He didn't have to dig so deeply, but he dug until his head had disappeared into the ground and the water would allow him to go no deeper.

Dolor and Dante buried all seven of the family they recovered, in this sandy grave by the ocean, across the washed out road, in front of their mother's shattered home. The seven are buried on the private land of Dr. Morabi, who does not know they are there.

Dolor and Dante swaddled the children in mats that they found buried in the ground, many mats, many kinds. A military man came by and helped them. Together the military man and Dante lowered the bodies using GI sheets and ropes.

At one point Dante had planned to transfer the bodies to the public cemetery and the tomb of Dolor's father, but the authorities have closed that cemetery. Dante has a friend in the National Bureau of Investigation (NBI) who offered to help bury the bodies at the Holy Cross Cemetery, but Dante is hesitating. He is okay with the bodies where they are, wrapped in blankets, near the sea.

One of the retrieval teams asked permission to move the bodies, but the Lingo's did not give them permission. When Dolor is lonely and alone—and these days, even among the many returning survivors, she is often lonely and alone—she goes to the graves, sits by the sea and talks to the ones buried there. The wind rustles her hair. She doesn't cry. She pushes her feet into the sand. She talks and talks. She hopes they will hear.

Dolor—one year later

For Dante and Dolor few things are as they were. The simple home they loved is long gone, washed out and blown away. They have a much more expensive home now. An international mission organization has built them a three-story house, with a rooftop balcony. It towers over the community, above the Hot Chile Factory. You can stand on the rooftop balcony and view all the empty shrimp pits that look like dominoes in a row. It has cost over one and a half million pesos and the neighbors think they are rich people.

They have been interviewed by national media organizations and featured in mission videos. Dante is now an ordained minister through the Multiplication Church Communities Seminary. He started training in February 2014, and was ordained August 2014. There is no salary, but there is much work to be done. Every Sunday Dante preaches and Dolor has a ministry feeding the children. Wednesday they lead prayer meetings, Tuesday a small group, Thursday bible study, and Friday teenager fellowship.

One week after the typhoon, Dante had a dream where he saw his children in the clouds. Daniel told him, "Don't worry Papa, we are happy now with the Lord. Enjoy your life with Mama and Dante Junior."

Dolor is no longer working for a "pre-need" company. None of her customers can pay for what they want to buy and so the business died.

Their life has been both blessed and cursed, but it is hard for Dolor to count the blessings and hard for Dante to acknowledge the curse. Nothing is easy. They, like sixty percent of their neighbors, have no income. They live day to day on extra food gleaned from the church.

When TV 7&4 came to interview them, Dante joked, "Do not interview my wife." He was unsure of what she would say. Not sure if she would give glory where glory was due or share sorrow where sorrow was found. But regardless of glory, sorrow, or something in-between Dolor is incredibly strong. She smiles, she serves, she cooks and cleans, she cares for her son. She overachieves in her service to the church.

Dante is impressed to be strong. He knows their life has been shattered, but he is challenged to share the gospel. The typhoon is still bringing converts. He sees craziness all around him, people who do not have God, no one to call on.

Dolor is a wave in the sea. It is something to have lost a family. She remembers them all: Mother, Constellation, Nenita, Auntie Jane, the nieces, nephews, and Carl, Daniel and Princess Diana. She remembers the laughter, the joy, their simple home, the big house, the busyness of her work and Dante's work, the beauty of the coconut palms along San Pedro Bay. She remembers all these things. She finds it is very hard to accept. She cannot help herself and so she questions everything she has understood to be good and true.

Dolor and Dante are serving. Sunday, Tuesday, Wednesday, Thursday and Friday, they are servers without salaries, volunteering to feed members of their community. But sadness envelops her. She knows, as everyone knows, that in a blink of an eye they will be gone. She accepts the fact that this is their life. She knows God is the owner and He must have a purpose, but she is unsure of His path for her life or His plan. The nearness of death and the quickness of death have made life seem small and immaterial.

She feels the dead who are buried near the ocean are eternal. She longs to be with them, floating in a sea of sand.

Beryl is swollen and her joints are sore to the point she cannot walk. Between the dengue and the chicken gonea, the aftermath of the typhoon is kicking up the debris and turning it into disease, like a cloud of dust from a dried round mushroom.

—From an aid worker's journal, 2014, Tacloban, Philippines

CHAPTER 4

A Sea of Sand

CARLITO QUIAS

I n the days that followed others saw Carlito. Allan Labita, a
former barangay official saw him. "He was a zombie," Allan
said. "He just walked around Barangay San Jose, no there,
there."

Carlito has one salvaged pedicab, but this pedicab came with a
high cost. Of the seventeen in their home at the time of the storm, only
seven survived. Willy, Claring's son who arrived just before the storm
and Carlito survived from the raft. Claring's sons Jun and Roning,
the two men who had come with Jun from the Astrodome, Jomer and
Erning, and Carlito's son, Rex, were all who were left of the twelve
who transferred to the barangay hall. None of the children and none
of the women lived. Of the nine that died, only baby Sunshine, carried
by Willy and Carlito, was found.

The pedicab has a sorry history. Willy had found the pedicab after
the typhoon in the possession of some looters. He had negotiated a
payment of one thousand pesos for it. Willy did not know Carlito had
survived. They first met near the Astrodome. It was a cold meeting.
Willy had Carlito's pedicab. Carlito did not have Willy's mother.
Carlito wanted his pedicab. Willy blamed Carlito for the loss of

his mother. Perhaps the ensuing anger and vitriol could have been mitigated had Carlito not demanded the pedicab, but in his words, "It is hard to let go of a pedicab. There is nothing left. Only the pedicab. It means a new start."

Not only could Carlito not let go, but he went to the police. When Willy heard about this he came to the Astrodome, where Carlito had evacuated. He kicked down Carlito's makeshift door, screaming and shouting at him. Carlito got his pedicab, but he made an enemy out of Willy. And Willy has been very vocal.

The nights are long and full of questions. Carlito experiences the typhoon again and again, reliving it over and over, until it is becoming more alive in his dreams than when it actually happened. He is trying to move on, to the next level, something he has always done, forgetting the past and starting over, but it has been harder this time.

He is living in a temporary shelter provided by the government. He has a room of his own in one of the many coconut lumber bunkhouses. There are twelve rooms in his bunkhouse, forty occupants, two toilets, no electricity, and no running water. He lives with people he does not know. He is expecting aid from the government. He expects compensation for the dead, though he has no legal relationship with the dead. He expects a six-month stipend. He expects all these things and in the meantime he does his job as a pedicab driver.

He remembers his father saying to avoid confrontations. His father had said, "Whatever you do will come back heavier than your action." It was a lesson Carlito's father learned through murder.

Today Carlito is trapped in a life he has made; one that Yolanda sharpened and simplified. It has come to a pedicab.

Carlito—a year later

Carlito is still living in one of the infamous Tacloban bunkhouses. His single room abuts up to other rooms, separated by quarter inch plywood on two by two framing. The tin roof and open rafters heat up his space like a boiler, radiating and spreading the sun's heat into the stifling, windowless interior. When Carlito lies on his mat on the floor, his thin body sweats and drips and the wooden platform around his mat is stained, as if it was done with a stencil.

His son Rex lives with him. Rex's wife Reah, the one hit by a piece of corrugated tin as the twelve transferred to the barangay hall was swept away and never found. She was pregnant with their first child.

Carlito found Rex a few days after running into Willy. It was a muted meeting.

"Rex, you are alive," Carlito had said. "Where is Reah?"

Rex just looked away his eyes red and watery. "Taken," he replied.

"Claring is gone. They are all gone," Carlito said.

Of the eight pedicabs Carlito had owned, besides the one he had confiscated from Willy, he found one more in the ocean.

To make peace, Carlito has given back to Willy the pedicab Willy had bought from looters, and Carlito had taken.

He found Willy and said, "Okay, I really want the pedicab, but if you want it you can have it." He was hoping Willy would let it go. The offer hung there a moment as Willy debated on anger without a pedicab or reconciliation with it.

"Okay," Willy replied. "If you really want me to have it, I will take it."

The two did not hug or shake hands. The pedicab was turned over, but Willy and Carlito are okay now.

Carlito is working. His new route is from the bunkhouse to the city hardware, back and forth. No longer is he traversing the side streets of San Jose. On a good day he will earn fifty pesos, just over a dollar. There are long waits for passengers. When he is not driving, Rex drives.

The narrow corridor between Carlito's row house is partially shaded by the wide overhangs. Women squat and nurse their children, do laundry, or talk across the three-meter path to other women standing hip to door. Children play, or sleep. The authorities arrange clean-up times and the survivors gather with makeshift tools—grass brooms, old shovels. Together the refugees make a show of cleaning and re-arranging. They then receive their allotment of rice and other staples.

Carlito is fitting into this life. He is making friends, the neighbors all know him. "Carlito, Carlito, oh yes he is in bunkhouse number twenty-one."

He remembers Claring saying, "If it is your time, it's your time." He is moving on. He has gone up to Samar to visit his second wife, Rosia. Who knows what will happen there.

"I am thankful I am still alive," he says. "For me I do not want to think about Yolanda anymore. It is done. It has happened. I have gone to church and everything I still have, I have given to God."

Yesterday, we ventured into the bowels of Barangay 88, an area called Baybay. Here it is as if the storm happened yesterday. There is tremendous need for clean up and feeding. The homes reach into the bay with the torn tentacles of families' belongings. In Baybay whole families were lost, swept off the perch of land they lived on like crumbs on a counter, washed into the water and swirled around until dead and for the most part buried, except for an occasional floater that bobbed along the shore as bait for the crabs. Crabs that we eat when we can afford them or find them. Baybay is a nest of tents and reclaimed sheet metal of all colors and sizes, quilted together to form a semblance of shelters, among the broken debris of past homes.

—From an aid worker's journal, 2014, Tacloban, Philippines

CHAPTER 4

A Sea of Sand

REGIE PAA

The water lay in huge pools. Regie climbed down from the twisted red iron of Kuya Boy's roof. It was 11:00 am Friday morning. He began to gather bottles of Coke and mineral water floating in the water. They had washed out of the Coke factory across the roundabout. Regie used a bottle of Coke to clean the mud and salt water off the stove burners and gas valves. He found saturated rice in the pantry. He rinsed it with mineral water. By 1:00 pm there was a stream of people in the streets. He borrowed a lighter from someone walking by. He cooked food for the family.

In the evening a man walked by with a megaphone warning about another tsunami. He was shouting into the megaphone. "Tsunami warning! Tsunami warning! Everyone must evacuate. Tsunami..."

The family took what they could find in the way of belongings. Regie had his phone, but his clothes were gone. They walked to Remedios Trinidad Romualdez (RTR) Hospital a few kilometers away. They and hundreds of others found shelter in the hills and high areas of Tacloban. The hospital was crowded, full of injured and shocked people. The family found spots to sleep, but sleep was limited. No one wanted to be caught napping with a wall of water coming like an army toward them. Regie stayed up most of the night. He stood with others, looking, watching, waiting.

The tsunami warnings were false. The night was long. Regie dozed off at 4:00 am, but woke at 6:00 am. It was Saturday morning. Kuya Boy handed him some money to buy rice. Regie went out and found rice at a little store north of the hospital.

"I would like to buy some rice," he said. He could see it on their shelves.

"No rice available we need the rice for ourselves," was the reply.

He haggled a bit, but the storeowners refused to sell, and Regie did not have the energy to argue. He returned to Kuya Boy and gave him his money back.

"No one wants to sell their rice," he said. "I am going out to see what I can find."

Regie went back to the car lot and the Coke plant. He found a jug of mineral water lying there and headed south on the Tabuan National Highway towards Robinson's mall and Palo. He wanted to see what, if anything, was available.

At the Marasbaras Church, just past Robinson's mall, the water was still three feet deep. He passed the Inglesia Ni Cristo Church and one person lay dead at its gate. At St. Peter's near the oval and Palo center, dead were everywhere, lying in bundles and makeshift rows. Hundreds of people were out, wandering and crisscrossing the streets. He saw a parade of people, many carrying bodies. They carried them on their heads and backs. They carried them on their bikes. They carried them in their arms.

At some point in this search for food and understanding, the real reason Regie had set off became known. He was going home. He had known he wanted to go home and he had told Bobby the helper to "Kindly tell Kuya Boy, I am going home to my family." But he didn't know for sure if it was a possibility.

The walk toward Palo was a scouting trip to see if there was transportation available. He talked to two policemen. "Can I find a ride to Biliran?"

One of the officers, dirty and haggard, responded by shrugging his shoulders and holding out his hands. "We don't know," he said. He pointed at the dead bodies that were coming from every direction. The policeman turned away as if confused.

Regie asked a few people about rides and damage. No one he asked could give a coherent answer. He started walking west on San Salvador Street, which turns into the Palo-Carigara-Ormoc City Road. With each step the urge to go became stronger. He walked faster and began to jog and then run. The horrors of the storm gave him wings. Wendell was dead. The car lot was gone. His only thought was for Bhe and his children. He ran a staggering, crisscrossing run, climbing over debris and slogging through mud. He was wearing a pair of gym shorts, t-shirt and rubber sandals. He wore the same clothes he had worn on Thursday evening when he crawled into the Toyota Crosswind and had fallen asleep. He had eaten one meal of rice. It was 6:30 am. He had not slept for twenty-four hours. He was filthy dirty. Black mud was caked on him and his clothes. He carried one thousand pesos in the battery area of his cell phone. He had a bottle of filtered water from the Coca-Cola plant.

He ran toward Santé Fe and out of Palo. The houses he passed were destroyed. Every house was roofless with shattered walls. Every tree was splintered and broken. He saw this as he ran and he kept thinking of his home in the mountains. All Regie could see was destruction.

He ran and he climbed over and under trees. He ran past hundreds upon hundreds of dead birds. They littered the road and made small soft molten mounds that when stepped on, they slipped under his sandals like rotten fruit. He ran past the cemetery in Alangalang, which was twenty-four kilometers from Tacloban. The four hundred year old mahogany trees in the cemetery were uprooted. Their branches, a tangle of limbs, sheltered the graves.

Regie bought three loaves of bread for sixty-six pesos in Alangalang. The storeowner appraised him. "How is it in Palo? he asked.

"Not good," said Regie. "Not good." He did not want to talk.

In the distance he saw two men walking. He caught up with them slowly. They were like him, survivors leaving Tacloban. He gave them one loaf of bread. When Regie ran on the other two joined him. The three ran together. When they were thirsty they would take coconuts scattered on the ground and break them with rocks. One of his new companions was an airport employee who had been on duty when the typhoon hit. He had seen the surge coming and had raced before it, looking for a place to climb, like a man running from a bear. He had reached a tree, climbing as the water tried to claw him down. He had climbed until he was half in the wind and half in the water, afraid to go higher, afraid to go lower. The airport was history. He too was going home.

In Tunga one of the duo dropped off, exhausted. The police were clearing the roads in Tunga, trying to make them passable for motor vehicles. Regie and the airport employee continued on, running, jogging, walking, staggering forward.

The two ran until they came to Carigara. At Carigara, Regie's legs began to cramp and he struggled to walk, much less run. The cramps centered just behind his knees, so he hobbled forward bent over and in pain. He had run fifty kilometers in just under four hours. It was ten-thirty Saturday morning, the day after the typhoon. He and his companion stopped at an intersection and waved at passers-by for a ride. It took hours for the first motorcycle to stop. Regie paid him one hundred pesos and the motorcycle transport took the two of them to Capoocan.

From Capoocan to Lemon. From Lemon to Biliran. From Biliran to the bridge in Leyte. A saga of waiting and paying for motorcycling rides. When Regie tried to walk his knees buckled. His airport companion had left him at Capoocan. The transportation was tortuously slow, traversing over and around fallen trees and debris. In Capoocan he waited three hours for a ride. His filthy clothes and body frightened people away.

When Regie passed the San Juanico Bridge he saw some green trees, the first green trees he had seen. There was still damage—houses destroyed, trees downed, flooding—but up until this point the landscape had been a brown wasteland, stripped of foliage. He walked from the San Juanico Bridge to Core Elementary School where his wife was teaching school. He walked very slowly, bent over, the cramps warping his legs into knots. He saw Bhe before she saw him. She was standing outside the school talking to a group of people. He came slowly, like an old man, but his heart was racing. He embraced her. She responded lamely, holding onto the worry for her children and her anger at Regie, but he didn't care. It was 7:00 pm, and just over one hundred and ten kilometers from the Coca-Cola plant. It had taken him thirteen hours.

"Bhe," he said. "Many people have died in Tacloban. Can I have something to eat?"

Regie told Bhe his story as he ate and people began to crowd around and listen. They gathered because of what he looked like and stayed to listen, because of what had happened. He told of the tsunami devastation on the eastern coast. Regie's was the first report from Tacloban. Radio and TV had been down since Friday morning. One of the listeners was Allan Labita's sister, Agnes, who lived in Biliran. She listened holding her breath, her hand on her throat, thinking of her sisters Tina, Aileen, Armida and her four brothers, and her mother, and all the others, praying for their safety.

Because of Regie's story, many residents of the area left for the coast to find family members.

Bhe and Regie hitched rides to Biliran. When they reached Bagacay Road it was closed. Trees were toppled. They got to their hillside forest homes at midnight, but there were no homes. They could see the empty space that should have silhouetted the houses.

"Mama!" Mama! Where are you? Where are you?" Regie called twice. The black forest held its breath and waited.

"Regie, your mother is in the pigpen," his aunt called from somewhere hidden.

Regie slept Sunday morning in the pigpen. He curled up with his wife, his two children, his father, his mother and the pigs. It was a concrete pen with three-foot sidewalls. There was a grass roof over it that his father had built to keep out the rain. He could hear the forest sounds. He could hear the breathing of his children and wife and the pig, or was that his dad? For the first time in three days he felt a semblance of peace, thankful to God.

The Bagacay Road—a road notorious for hold-ups—winds up to this mountainous village. The home is traversed only by a path chopped through the foliage. The Paa family compound, destroyed by Yolanda, months later has a row of flowers lining its path. Stumps have been hollowed out and small bouquets planted in each one. Here there is still shade from the coconut trees, unlike in Tacloban.

This is where Regie lives now, where he had walked and run, never resting, to get to. He has planted a variety of raised beds. They are meticulously weeded. He has built a small shelter for his family. He remembers the typhoon as if it was yesterday. He remembers his boss calling from Cebu after the typhoon telling him to transfer the cars.

Regie had told him. "They are floating already." This is the last correspondence he has had from his boss or from Tacloban. He assumes that his closest friend Wendell had drowned. Regie has not heard from Kuya Boy's family, the family he saved. It has been four months and he has no desire or motivation to leave the province.

Regie's sister, Aggie, lost her husband in Yolanda. They were washed out in San Jose. Her husband had saved her and their child, expending everything he had. A silent hero swept into eternity. She spends her time on the mountain, the baby cradled on her hips.

His mother, the matriarch of this place, is lobbying hard for aid. She is pressuring Regie, something she is good at, but Regie does not seem to hear. He just smiles at his mother and goes about his day. The matriarch is beside herself. She has driven her husband, a man with no teeth, she has driven her children. And now Yolanda had come along and usurped her, trumped her with a stronger hand.

His mother cannot understand the change Yolanda has caused in Regie. He is different. He will not leave the mountain. He will not communicate with her. He isn't providing as he has provided for many years. She is impatient with the situation. She is impatient, but she is afraid to let her impatience show. She isn't sure how Regie will respond.

They have a saying among Regie's hills, "Rocks for relief." The local mayor provides relief goods, but only if they are traded for rocks. The rocks are re-building the bridges in Tacloban, Palo and throughout Leyte. Regie hasn't gathered rocks. He does not intend to. His mother would, but she is too old.

Regie—a year later

One year later, Regie's hair is longer. His eyes are still kind, but a haunted kind. He has not worked a regular job. His slippers (flip-flops) are banded together with wire stitches. "I am very much destroyed," he says.

"I share food with my mother's house if we do not have enough. We have even visited our mother-in-law to eat food there. My school records are destroyed and I have no money to get new ones." The cost of new records or transcripts is thirty-five hundred pesos. He needs those to apply for "good" jobs, jobs that pay over the minimum of two hundred pesos a day.

"We have no budget for milk so we are buying Milo (a chocolate malt powder mixed with water) for the kids. We give one half a serving to our two-year-old. We just add sugar to make up the difference. My gardening is providing *ampalaya* (bitter gourd), string beans, but it is not enough."

His wife, Bhe, was a substitute teacher, but that was a temporary job. For years she has been trying to get a teaching position in the public schools, but it is a rigged system. "You had to know somebody to get appointed," said Regie.

They don't know anybody.

Bhe is from Cebu, half Waray and half Cebuano. She graduated from Naval State University with honors. She is a good teacher and on the yearly rankings, which she is required to pay for at a cost of thirty-five hundred pesos she scores well. When there are job openings, the applicants are ranked according to their annual scores, but these rankings mean little when it comes to actual jobs. The Mayor is allowed two appointments, regardless of qualifications, and CHED (Commission on Higher Education) is allowed eight. Jobs are given on a friendship basis.

Bhe is angry about it. "Why is God letting this happen to us?" she asked Regie. "I do not know what to do. What should I do?"

These questions hang like smoke in the air of their home. They are hazy questions with choking answers. The money they need for Regie to get his transcripts and Bhe to get her annual certification is out of their reach. Things were difficult before Yolanda, but today the weight seems unbearable. Bhe's willowy frame, taller than Regie's, and his slight body, but strong, are bending, cracking and slowly breaking down. The children are hungry.

"Fuck the CHED," says Regie. "Burn it down. The requirements, the P3,500 they want for licenses. Borrowing money for this joke of a system, so some politician can appoint his friend. Every year P3,500! Maybe this is God's will. Maybe in His time, but this is not a godly institution. This is inhumane."

Yolanda has stretched their family. Regie was one of the heroes, which is a matter of circumstance and character, but heroism is not a blank check. It is not any check at all. Regie does not think about it or feel it. He just feels an incomprehensible emptiness and longing to feed his family and recover the joy he once had.

It seems like forever since the day Yolanda came, the time of laughter with his closest friend Wendell is long gone. Peek-a-boo, their childish game, vanquished by the surge.

There are those who would celebrate my choices, and I have heard that often enough. But it is the celebrated words I most mistrust. They comfort and satiate me and in their listening the red wine tastes better and better as I drink it down like water until I find myself drunk and spinning and ultimately useless to the world around me. It is only in painful criticism and the quietness of aloneness that I can find words I trust and can learn from. The smallness of this part of my life is frightening. When the celebrations overwhelm the silence, then the life of man will disappear and be lost forever.

—From an aid worker's journal, 2014, Tacloban, Philippines

C H A P T E R   4

A Sea of Sand

D A N A   L A B I T A

Friday afternoon, Jean, the other nurse, and Dana began to survey the area around them from the window. Dana could not believe what she was seeing. It looked like the end of the world. Dr. Lay was sitting in her chair with a blank look on her face. Dana felt blank too. She did not think about her family, only the present; it was all the reality she could bear.

"Dana, Dana, we will have lunch now." It was Doctor Lay.

Dana was shocked. It took a while for the word to register. She was not hungry. "What time is it?"

"It is three o'clock Dana."

Seven hours had passed. They ate muddy biscuits and water.

"How are your children?" Dr. Lay asked.

"Okay," she answered. And then as if the question had sparked some distant memory, prompting a forgotten remembrance, the seed of motherhood began to grow and she thought that she needed to go to the children. She could not think why, but the thought kept nagging at her and finally she asked Dr. Lay if she could go. "May I go home to my family?" She asked.

"Okay," the Doctor said. "But please return. We are old and do not know what to do."

It was 4:10 pm Friday afternoon when Dana left. She knew that because her wristwatch was still functioning. She walked by Gaisano Super Market. There were crowds of people gathered there. Dana was not sure why there were so many people. She was confused as well by the wounded people she saw, some with fractures.

She passed by Sacred Heart Church. It looked like it had been vacuumed out. The saints were gone. The pews were gone. The doors were gone. She prayed as she passed. "Thank you for saving us." She walked by Santo Niño Church. It was crumpled in places, and it too looked vacuumed out. It seemed like a washing machine had scattered all the chairs. The saints were gone there as well. She prayed again. "Thank you for saving us. My family and me."

She walked along Real Street, past the Astrodome, going to San Jose. It started to rain, a steady drizzle. She was seeing sights and trying to piece them together in her mind, trying to take what her eyes were feeding her and scrub them into focus. She saw people coming from San Jose. She saw wounded and dead people on the road, injuries everywhere, children, mothers, people crying. Her mind could not absorb it. She could not rinse the thick soap off the images, but she tried, like digging out of a drug-induced sleep, she fought to understand.

Someone recognized her and called. "Ate Dana, Ate Dana, Ax is missing."

Dana heard her. She began to cry out. "God, I will not permit anything to take Ax away from us. Ax, stay where you are. Mama is coming." Then she collapsed in the gutter and tried to understand why someone would speak the words to her that Ax is missing.

Someone else recognized her and told her that her parents were safe. Her parents lived in San Jose, near Allan and her home. She felt assured and got up.

She walked past the round-a-bout where the Coca-Cola plant had been and turned toward San Jose. She was amazed at the sediment and destruction. She kept repeating the words, "Mama is coming, wait, mama is coming." Over and over she repeated these words as she walked against a river of people. Hundreds of people were streaming out of San Jose; the road was thick with people and wreckage. She had to climb over ruins. She could see dead bodies everywhere, lying brown and gray. It was getting dark and Dana decided she must walk back and forth across the road so as not to miss her family because everyone was coming out.

Allan and Dana met outside their home on the DZR Highway. He half-carried, half-dragged her to the counselor's home where many from their barangay had taken refuge. The first night was long and painful. Darkness and grief merged into a quiet hell. In the morning the counselor's wife was overheard yelling to her husband.

"Get them out of here. They will ruin my house."

No one heard the counselor's response.

"Feed them some hotdogs and get them out."

Dana's spirit as a mother and as a person living in poverty had no place for inhumane meanness. The dignity and strength that was inherent to her life was restored by the weakness and indecency of the counselor and his wife. She became a mother and a provider again. At 6:00 am Saturday morning, everyone who had sought refuge in the counselor's mansion left.

Saturday at 12:00 pm, Dana and Allan decided to relocate the children, Phil, Yugi, and Bridgette to her parent's home. Allan was constantly looking for Ax, but Dana refused to search among the dead. Her parents lived a few kilometers south toward the MacArthur monument, near the San Jose High School. The road to her parents was thick with people, still dazed, in shock and in many cases injured. Dana's childhood home was gone. The old trees that had stood in her yard were uprooted and tumbled upon each other, but her family had survived. She hugged her brother, a person she loved, but never hugged. This hug was a bridge built from Yolanda emotion. Yolanda gave plenty of emotion, doling it out with inclusive generosity.

The smell of death in her parents' area was overwhelming. It was sweet and putrid at the same time. The lack of sleep, the long walk—it was two kilometers to Dana's mothers—the death, the piles of debris, the mud, the heat, the lack of food, the children, menstruation—Dana, Tina, and Allan's niece all were menstruating out of their cycle—took superhuman strength, strength she did not have, but somehow found. Dana and Allan realized the children could not stay at her mother's, so they left to walk directly to the morgue. They were stopped by a neighbor who informed them that Allan's mother had been found. She was found upside down, her feet pointing to the sky, her face buried in the mud.

The short hours after Yolanda turned into unending hours, a struggle for shelter, for food, for water, for sanitation and for hope. Dana's community was a teeming caldron of destroyed lives, with no reserve. Many people in the neighborhood approached Allan and Dana—she, because she was a nurse and Allan because he was a former barangay official, but also because they were there and had a semblance of composure. Dana's composure had to overcome the smell and feel of her own clothes leaking blood. It was composure drawn from an inner resource. She was surrounded by chaos. Control of that chaos was not something their circumstances allowed.

There was the hour in which they passed by Mercury Drug, a national chain of drug stores. They were going to the morgue with their good friend Chairman Leo Bahin. The doors to Mercury Drug were open and it was being looted. Without thinking Dana pushed her way in. She found milk and diapers. It was not easy. She had the diapers between her knees and a milk container in each arm. She had to fight to get out. It was so crowded she was "losing air "and she realized she was the only woman there. Allan and the chairman asked why she was looting and she replied, "I am getting milk for my babies."

There was the hour she met the mayor and the vice mayor. They asked where she was coming from. She told them San Jose. They asked what she needed and she told them medicines. They gave her two cases of medicine and tetanus injections. She became a clinic, distributing medicine and giving tetanus shots.

There was the hour Uncle Alex died, from a stroke and a laceration, but before he did there were hours that Dana nursed and comforted him.

There were hours on the road to Biliran, to stay with Allan's sister, who had come to Tacloban after hearing a report from Regie Paa, a used car salesman who worked across from the Coca-Cola plant.

When Dana, the children, and Allan's remaining family fled the city with Allan's sister, the truck ran out of gas and they were stranded for four hours in a soaking rain. She cried helplessly as her children shivered.

There was the hour she heard that Allan had found Ax, but that was twelve days after Yolanda. It was a Tuesday.

When she returned from Biliran, she and Allan repaired their home. A few concrete pillars still stood, though precariously. Together the two of them fashioned a roof and some walls, and salvaged mother's easy chair. Just the two of them. They cleaned off some saints. The family—Allan, Dana, their children Phil, Yugi, and Bridgette, Allan's brothers, Kim, Arnel, Arman and Allan's sister's, Armida and Tina— moved back in, ten in all.

She and Allan have not stopped since Yolanda. More than ever before her immediate and extended family need a mother. Life is not normal. It is anything but normal. She is working for the Chinese women again. Her patient is still comatose and still alive. These are normal things, but nothing is the same. Her job seems unimportant to her. Time with her children is paramount.

The loss of Ax has changed her. She is less accepting of social rules that hinder survival. Yolanda was enough to survive. She is less willing to bow down and accept hunger as her birth inheritance. She is trying to understand God. She believed in His divine protection for her family. She had to believe this to temper the inequity society handed out, but now she has released that belief. She is trying to find the balance in her mind between faith and justice.

Occasionally she lights some candles to the saints.

Dana—one year later

If you take third street off DZR Highway and follow it deep into the community on broken, half-paved roads and continue until the confused mass of life thins out and the road becomes a two-track, you will eventually come to a small enclave, which is Dana and Allan's countryside home. She calls it "the farm". They have two pigs, a growing garden, a two-room bungalow, with a spacious open floor plan. There is an ocean breeze that filters through the thickening foliage to the house.

The "farm" is in the San Jose District, near the base of the Peninsula. It is inherited land.

Yolanda has changing everything in Dana's life, her home, her job, her extended family, her goals, even her faith.

She has quit her job as a nurse. She is home with her children—Phil, Yugi and Princess Bridgette—the garden, the two dogs and Allan when he is not working. "When I quit the Lay sisters, they said they would just wait for me," she says, though she has no intention of going back.

The house built on inherited land is part cement, part hollow block, part coconut lumber and part salvaged tin. There is a bamboo fence that encircles the property. For the most part she and Allan built it themselves, as they had built Allan's mother's structure after the storm, but this is much different. For the first time in their married lives they live as a family unit without brothers, sisters and nieces or nephews rooming with them. There is an element of privacy in their lives.

Dana's parents are closer to her now than ever before. When she first married Allan, she was working overseas in Saudi Arabia. Her parents detested Allan. They considered him a gold digger, partially because they were gold diggers themselves. But Yolanda has taken away their desire for material things. Ax was a favorite of theirs. "When Ax was taken, everyone hurt, all the family, everyone opted to comfort and console. To say sorry takes a lot of nerve," said Dana. "It is something our President could learn."

In one corner of Dana's home are the saints. Dana's mother gave them the Jesus of Nazarene. A friend gave a beautiful statue of Mama Mary to them. He had seen it standing on the shore, alone, for days after Yolanda. Santo Niño, Young Jesus, was a statue Dana and Allan bought in Quiapo, Manila, in 2009; it survived Yolanda. And lastly, the Black Jesus had been found stuck in some debris.

Before the typhoon, before even her marriage to Allan, she was two persons. "I was Dana the clown, Dana the nurse, Dana the friend. I was always smiling, but inside I was homesick, missing my family. In my own bedroom I was Dana, but only to myself."

Dana is all of those things today and she is herself too.

"I have been told I am no longer a good Catholic, because I practice my own faith. A good Catholic will go to church every Sunday, attend the Rosary on Friday and pray to the saints. I have learned in a Catholic school and they want us to show outward expressions. This is no longer important to me. I do not attend Mass on a regular basis. Allan and I just stop into the place of worship when we pass by and I pray in the bathroom and in the kitchen…"

In Yolanda Dana felt tested by God. She was strong and thought that was a good thing. Now she is not so sure. Now she is glad simply to have survived.

Ax never leaves her mind. He is part of her flesh and her consciousness as a mother, but she wonders if perhaps he was a seven-year angel, a gift to help her grow.

This is a city washed out to sea and the result is disaster and death, yet now the stars can be seen again. Two months with no streetlights, stadium lights or house lights and even our stars would be seen again. Not seeing the stars, as I did as a child, is like not seeing eternity, like taking away dreams. From my window I think that maybe Tacloban will get its dream back if they look in silent awe at the heavens. It may be worth the loss of the power grids and for people to live as we have for the past three months so our children can see stars again.

—From an aid worker's journal, 2014, Tacloban, Philippines

AID WORKER'S JOURNAL

The Philippines is like a curtain to an inner chamber for me. I step on its soil, like pulling aside a blanket on a door, and God is there, holy, stern, loving, challenging, hopeful and fun.

My wife Deborah and I spent six years working in Manila, 2002-04 and 2007-2010, founding an organization called Urban Opportunities for Change Foundation, Inc., a long winded name because non-profits are a field of weeds in the Philippines, overgrown and proliferating. We had to keep adding and changing words till Urban was born. For four years we worked with a wonderful group of Filipinos publishing the *Jeepney Magazine* as a member of the International Network of Street Papers and organizing the Philippine Homeless World Cup Team. We had this idea of changing the lives of destitute people, through simple things such as jobs and play.

I remember Manila as a massive sprawling beast of a city, and people everywhere. Men with shirts tucked between bellies and breast, drinking and gambling. Women squatting over tubs of soapy water, children with a stick and a tire. The construction, towers of cranes dotting the skylines, the tradesmen living in huts in the rising shadows, the sweltering heat, and the sprawling malls with large packed corridors and people in uniforms. The traffic, the water, the rain, the air, which is often easier to see than the smoke. The jeepneys, the office where we worked day after day, and our friends too numerous to mention, but whose faces dot across the peripherals of my vision, and I remember them all fondly and even longingly.

I wrote this manuscript to help me understand a Filipino tragedy. Typhoon Haiyan caught my wife and me by surprise. We were not watching the news or checking Facebook. It was three days after the storm when emails began arriving and we realized this storm, one of the most powerful ever to hit landfall, had decimated Tacloban and the surrounding areas. My wife Debbi, sent an email to our former mission director, asking, "How can we help?"

"Get over here," he said.

We arrived in Tacloban ten days after the storm, November 17, 2013. A team of Filipinos from Kids International Ministries (KIM) was already there, providing what aid they could with limited resources. The day we arrived was the day the first of the shipping containers of dried sealed "manna packs" arrived at the Tacloban City dock. Before we left four months later over one million meals had been delivered through Kids International Ministries and somehow they had been cooked, fed, or distributed to thousands of people and one hundred plus churches and organizations.

In November and into December we slept on the second floor of the New Life Baptist Church. The first morning we woke up covered with mosquito bites. I looked at Debbi and said, "What's wrong with your face?"

"What's wrong with your face?" she retorted.

There was one bathroom for the survivors and one for the aid workers, shared by 20-40 of us. We took cold bucket showers, used a single latrine, and occasional confrontations erupted when the line grew long. We slept in tents on concrete in the empty washed out sanctuary, or in the classrooms on the first floor, but those rooms were often relegated to the snorers, which some thought I was. The cooking started at 4:00 am and the last of the deliveries were finished at 6:00 pm, when the blackness of the night and the curfew, shut the city down.

Eventually some of our group moved to the heavily damaged STEFTI school, built by one of Urban's board members, Dan Palami. We set up our tents in classrooms, large tiled rooms. The school courtyard was thick with Yolanda's sludge, and in the gutters outside the school wall pigs floated for weeks and then months. We smelled death in the swales surrounding us, but STEFTI was palatial compared to the vast majority of the city, and even the New Life Baptist Church.

When the school re-opened in late January—two and one-half months after the typhoon—we moved to the Palami family home, which also had been heavily damaged and flooded. For two months we worked out of the Palami home, distributing food, building coconut lumber homes, managing relief teams, scouting for a long-term KIM building. At night one of the Palami brothers ran an ice operation and the large generator would bellow and shudder into the wee morning.

The early mornings, and the late nights were filled with laughter. It may seem odd to have laughter in the midst of tragedy, like laughing at a funeral, but I have laughed in funerals before and will most likely laugh again. We had to laugh. It didn't mute the tragic, but it made it bearable. Occasionally we went to the beach and smoked a cigar and drank cheap rum.

I settled into a routine at the Palami home. Before the teams arose, I made coffee with a French press, sat in a cast iron garden chair, at a cast iron table, read a selection from "My Utmost for His Highest," by Oswald Chambers, my favorite, and wrote for thirty minutes. It was the only minutes of the day that were mine. When the teams arose I had a list of who went where. Who was driving, who was cooking, building, delivering, unloading at the docks, making the airport runs, buying and cooking the food for lunch and dinner, cleaning and all the details I suppose aid agencies do and deal with.

Debbi and I slept in a room with two others. We had a double bed on the second floor and another double bed was crammed next to ours. The two windows in the room were broken and the frames bent.

We had four cooking locations. One at New Life Baptist Church in Palo. One at STEFTI, School. One at the bay, in a damaged hotel next to the Foundation of Dan Palami, and one more in Tacloban at the residence of the Navigators. Eventually we moved the Foundation's feeding operation to Dan's uncle's property. We cooked in massive pots over open fires, adding ginger, garlic and onions to the rice and beans of the manna packs. We had six vehicles, two old Toyota vans, one green, one red, a Toyota Revo, one flatbed truck and for a few weeks one massive jeepney and one dump truck. Each day we fed up to six thousand survivors, mostly children. We had this illogical, but functioning, ever transitioning team, of nurses, social workers, cooks, drivers and survivors. We fed and we listened. We heard over and over, "I am a survivor, my story is long."

I remember a late evening. I was walking by a survivors' tent, the flap open, a man was lying, his feet toward me. I stopped. His legs looked rotten. It was past 6:00 pm when the sun disappears and darkness envelops the earth. We made our way to the German medical aid camp two kilometers down the road.

"Can it wait till morning?" the doctor asked. She had been showering.

"No." I said. And so they came with us, packed into our car, three Germans with their gear, my wife Debbi, Chris, and myself. We crept slowly back, because the landmarks had disappeared and our headlights only chipped a crack of visibility. It was good that Sel had scraped off the window tints from our cars. Between the lifeless street-lights and the tints you drove blind.

"We made our way along a river to the tent, where the family was waiting. The German doctor gave him morphine, and to us she said, "He needs his legs amputated, but I do not think he will survive it." Then she wrapped his legs and said she would come back in the morning.

A few days later the man died, but he died without pain, swaddled in clean bandages. It was all people could do. It was all we could do.

Dengue Fever hit us eventually. I have no idea how many cases there were in the city and surrounding areas, but over the course of our last month, at least twenty of our revolving team ended up with dengue.

At the Palami home we went around and poured gallons of bleach in the stagnant fish ponds and standing water. The community we were surrounded by was a mass of puddles, black refuse water, sewage water, human feces and dog shit.

The air was as stagnant as the water. There are tunnels between one and two story buildings, the openings peering out into the street. In the days of electricity and fresh water, a waterfall and tropical plants made the Palami home a sanctuary from the street. Four months after Yolanda it became a den of larvae. This is where I sat and wrote each morning. My place of refuge, coated with an invisible film of Deet.

When Debbi got sick I made arrangements for a three day visit to a resort on the Southern tip of Samar, one-hundred and sixty-five kilometers south, out of the storm damage. We drove six hours to get there. Debbi had wanted to go to Manila and rest in a hotel, but I could not imagine inspiration and recovery by trading the natural beauty of Leyte, for the decadence of a Makati hotel. So I agreed to the respite, but on my terms.

We found a place, a drive by, after rejecting the first resort. I do not remember either name. I remember the sound of the waves crashing. The only sound I heard in the night. Our room was ten meters from the shore, facing east on Sogod Bay. I remember the waves as a choppy Lake Michigan wave, bundled together like cords of knotty wood. They crashed against the rocks in a constant tumult of unremitting sound. Across Sogod Bay a mountainous shore rose into the clouds in shadowy grey layers.

For three days we lay there on the white sheets, in a white room, with wide glass doors looking at the blue water and the sun rising and shadowing the sea, until the dengue passed by and was gone, or in my case just starting in.

Tacloban seemed so far away, so forgotten those three days. The darkness of human sediment that covered Tacloban's earth was only a memory. Our comrades still serving, still feeding, still comforting, I barely remembered. Chris with a mop of hair, Jake with a quiet smile, Sel always serving, who were they now? This is what I thought would happen in Michigan. Tacloban would fade away.

I imagined sitting on a Brady's bar stool in Traverse City, Michigan and thinking about it all. But not much. It was easy to forgot everything, with the sea, the wind, the sky and my wife curled in the bed, in our little white room, her head toward the open double door, where the sounds were reaching her and caressing her, restoring her needy body and soul.

Out of this short time of respite, came this book, voices that needed to be heard and remembered. A project I could immerse myself in, and remember the land, the waters, and life on this earth, to be with, and stay with, people I love and care for, to understand the tragic mix of poverty and disaster. I suppose I wrote it for myself.

I met Allan Labita, through his sister Tina. Tina worked at the Palami Foundation, and was part of our feeding collaboration. Tina was a survivor, and like all the survivors, she worked and laughed along with us, as she fed, clothed and helped her community.

Tina introduced me to her brother Allan. We delivered "Manna Packs" to Allan and the broken down home of his mothers'. Allan's wife Dana was there, the three children, and one brother, suffering deeply, silent and troubled, so unlike a Filipino. I talked about a book with Allan and asked if I could interview him.

In Allan's broken down home, during the last two weeks of our Tacloban stay, we built a friendship. He became translator, guide, and listener, as together we sat and heard stories and interviews, not all used. Often our listening became therapy. I remember one story where the telling became a re-enactment, and Debbi, who was there too, took over with comfort, while I strode around the Palami courtyard and tried to shake off the anguish.

The three of us, Allan, Debbi and I, dedicated our later mornings to interviews. We would pick Allan up around 9:00 am, drive to a waiting survivor, find a safe place to conduct an interview, often in the Palami courtyard, but in other places too, like Samuel's seaside shelter, or Regie's mountain enclave. There we would listen, ask questions and I would take notes. Allan would say, "Oh my god, Oh my god." Or I remember when Regie's mom was lobbying for payment of some sort, he gently inserted that, "I am a survivor too. I too have lost."

And then I came home, back to Michigan, back to snow, back to house projects, community projects and family. I wrote the manuscript and then set it aside for a year, then started again, returned to Tacloban in the spring of 2015, wrote some more.

This book is a small window into the lives of seven people. Four months after the storm shock had turned into grief. But poverty does not lend itself easily to grief. In Dolor's case she purposed to show no emotion, and she didn't, for a time.

It was important to me that the stories be told as broken and real as life itself. I believe those who shared are satisfied that it is so and I am glad to be part of its telling.

For me the images of Allan and his gun, of Dolor and her peaceful home, of Regie a year later, broken and broke, of Carlito and his pedicab, of Samuel and his boat, of Noel the convict, and of Dana a mother, are forever embedded in my mind and thoughts. They represent all that is good and too much that is bad about a country we love and a land they live on.

William Shaw

This book could not have happened without Allan Labita. He was the first person we interviewed and became a confident and translator. His story is heroic, yet there is little victory in the death of a child.

Samuel Magdua, fisherman and survivor, reflects on Yolanda. We interviewed Samuel on the shores of Cancabato Bay, Barangay 88, in a makeshift home he had constructed. While telling his story he fought back tears as he struggles to process. "When I hear the word Yolanda I cry," he said.

Samuel's wife Geraldine observes Samuel as he speaks. Their relationship, always rocky, was restored after Yolanda

Samuel Magdua checks his boat one year after Yolanda. His green and white banka is anchored in the background. The trash at his feet is representative of his community. This land is owned by an influential political family and aid has been minimal.

These were the scenes that met the author
and photographer on their arrival in
Tacloban November 17th, 2013.

This photo was taken in November 2013 less than two weeks after Yolanda, but four months later bodies were still being pulled from the debris.

On Sunday afternoon the Labita family makes a weekly pilgrimage to the burial place of Ax. Uncle Alex, Aileen, baby Coleen and Allan's mother—all lost in Yolanda— are buried here. On this particular day Allan's sister Tina had already been to the graves and left flowers. Phill, Dana's oldest son is pictured.

This photo of Dana Labita was taken at the Palami home in
Tacloban. She shared the unbearable, which combined her
isolation as a former Overseas Filipino Worker (OFW), with
the loss of a son.

Noel Lito sings his song—Four kinds of Love—one of many he wrote in the Tacloban City Jail. The inmates were released from the Tacloban City Jail after the food and water ran out.

Noel Lito (alias) exposes a jail tattoo, one of many. He was one of the notorious at-large escapees listed on the airport wall when we arrived in Tacloban. At the time of this book's publishing he is still at-large with a shoot-to-kill order on his head. He had been incarcerated for five years for stealing a cell phone and yet to have a trial.

Just north of the Astrodome, remnants of Yolanda remain…

Cancabato Bay and the Astrodome are in the
background. The storm surge that destroyed this
home first had to sweep across Barangay 88, the
Daniel Z. Romualdez airport and Cancabato Bay.

Dolor Lingo, with Allan in the background, purposed to tell her story stoically without emotion. It wasn't possible.

The gravesite of seven of Dolor Lingo's family, including her children Carl, Daniel and Princess Diana. Dolor and her husband Dante keep the site simple hoping it will be undisturbed by the authorities.

Carlitos Quios pauses while telling of his terrifying
journey through the dark waters of Yolanda. He was
swept across the base of Cancabato Bay on the floor
of a house.

Regie's wife Bhe, and her children reside in their provincial compound. She listened to Regie's story from a distance saying little.

Regie Paa and two-year-old son Naphanien, Regie tells a harrowing tale of destruction, and of his 120 kilometer trek from Tacloban to Biliran.

Found hidden along Maharlika Highway in Palo, this man's shelter became a regular stopping point for the Kids International Ministries' food deliveries. His wife and children were dead. It was not uncommon for men to survive and their families die. The living are struggling still, waiting to heal, trying to understand.

Photographer Deborah Shaw, pausing for a moment of pleasure.

The last day the author was in Tacloban, March 5th, 2014. This photo was taken 100 feet from Samuel's home on Cancabato Bay. Samuel was the last person we interviewed, a day before we left. I really wanted to get a feel of the community, the water, the air, the smells and noises. I assume this had been someone's kitchen, with a window overlooking the water and Tacloban in the distance.